New Reality: Truth

Michael Robertson

Website and Newsletter:
http://michaelrobertson.co.uk

Email: subscribers@michaelrobertson.co.uk

New Reality: Truth
Michael Robertson
© 2014 Michael Robertson

New Reality: Truth is a work of fiction. The characters, incidents, situations, and all dialogue are entirely a product of the author's imagination, or are used fictitiously and are not in any way representative of real people, places or things.

Any resemblance to persons living or dead is entirely coincidental.

DEDICATION

And then there were four. Amy, Seb, and Marcie, you're my reason for being. Your support and understanding make my writing possible.

To anyone who has downloaded this book. Thank you.

Prologue

Jake groaned as he kneeled down next to the inert woman. A year of poor diet and exposure to the elements had left him feeling like a rusty hinge. He felt the weight of the machete as long as his forearm in his right hand; its perfect balance made it feel like an extension of his body. In a world where everything was battered to within an inch of its life—and often beyond that—the polished blade still looked brand new.

"I'm not sure about this!" Tom shouted over the gale force winds, the scarf covering his mouth muffling his voice. "What if she twitches while you're doing it?"

"She won't," Jake said, scanning their surroundings. The dust storm reduced visibility to about fifty metres. He looked back at Tom, who was so tense he was brittle, and waited for him to say more. When Tom was in this frame of mind, there was always more.

"And what will we do about Rixon?"

Bingo.

"They'll be on top of us before we know it."

A moth of anxiety fluttered in Jake's chest and he searched the flattened wasteland again.

"That's why we need to be quick."

The statement was as much for himself as it was for Tom. Complacency in this world led to death. Swallowing, Jake grimaced from the burn of the grit in his throat. The dust got everywhere, regardless of the rag covering his mouth. Shaking his head, he squinted as he looked into the storm. "How do they always know what we're doing?"

Tom raised his slim shoulders in a shrug that ran the length of his beanpole body. "They see everything."

"You're paranoid."

Standing taller, Tom's face twisted at Jake's comment. "So what if I am? My paranoia has saved us on more than one occasion over this past year."

Jake rolled his eyes. "Keep your knickers on, sweetheart. I'm just playing with you. Seriously though, once we start this, the clock will be ticking. No fucking about. You got that?"

The long nose and dour expression on Tom's face made him look like he belonged in a stable.

"The point I'm trying to make," Jake said, "is that we don't have time for sentimentality." Standing up, he rubbed the top of Tom's left arm. It felt like rubbing a sleeved stick. "I appreciate this must be hard for you, but you need to keep your head. We need to get her out of New Reality before they get to us."

Tom didn't respond.

Sighing, Jake shook his head. "I can't believe it was only a year ago when they levelled the city. I can't believe we both decided to hide by the Rixon Tower. We probably never would have met if we hadn't."

Standing up had sent sharp needles of pain into Jake's hip. Wincing, he rubbed the sore area. "It feels like much longer."

Bending down, Tom swiped away some of the surface debris from the woman's body. "It looks like she's been here for much longer too."

It was the first time Jake had met Tom's wife. She was so fat she looked like she was melting into the environment. What did Rixon gain from making the gamers obese? Was it to make them die quicker? To give them less people to be responsible for? It wasn't murder if their bodies failed them.

With skin so pale it was virtually translucent; Jake shuddered at the sight of the varicose veins that streaked across her fat arms. Watching Tom for a moment as he removed small pieces of brick and concrete, he put a hand on his friend's skinny shoulder. "We'll get the headset off, mate. I'm sure she'll be fine."

Tom stopped what he was doing and looked up at his friend; his eyes glazed with tears. The confidence with which Jake had delivered his statement had already vanished. Looking at the woman again, he pointed at the headset. It was made from glossy black plastic and had a red stripe running across it. The stripe bore the name of its creator—Rixon.

"If I never see another one of these again, it'll be too soon," he mumbled.

Tom didn't reply.

The headset was probably a perfect fit three years ago but now it looked like it belonged to someone half her size. Her ever-expanding body had partly consumed the plastic headpiece much the same way as a tree grows around an iron fence until they become one. Looking at how tight it was on her head made a pulse throb in Jake's temples. Trying to rub his headache away did nothing. "She looks like she's in a coma."

Another glare from Tom made Jake raise his hands in defence. "Sorry, mate, but she does."

"Can you please call her by her name?"

"Sorry... Thalia; I didn't mean to disrespect you."

Regarding Tom again, Jake added, "Rixon claims she's in paradise now." He scanned their surroundings—no Bots. "That headset is allowing her to experience her dreams on every level." Jake used his fingers to count. "Sight, sound, touch, taste, smell."

"Right—five-dimensional entertainment; what's your point, Jake?"

"My point is that she looks fu—" Tom's scowl cut him short. "She doesn't look like she's living any kind of fantasy life."

After clearing the last of the debris away from her chest, Tom pointed at the headset. "What will happen when we pull this thing off?"

"There's only one way to find out. Are you sure you want to try?"

Although his face was creased with worry lines as he searched their environment, Tom nodded. "I have to. She's my wife. They don't fucking own her."

After clearing his throat, Jake said, "Right, you ready?"

All Tom managed was another weak nod.

When Jake knelt down, his knees burned like the joints were filled with broken glass. Biting down on his bottom lip, he stifled a moan; Tom didn't need to hear how much he was hurting. Not today. Not now.

Black straps held the headset in place and dug into her flabby neck. Taking a deep breath, Jake slid his index finger along her pallid and waxy skin, but he couldn't get beneath the straps. The strain was so tight on them, the pressure could crack nuts. Probing farther, Jake's long fingernail nicked her flesh and she stared to bleed.

"Be careful, Jake," Tom hissed.

Finally getting purchase on one of the straps, Jake pulled it away from her neck and exposed a gap of just a few centimetres. When he slid the shiny blade of the machete into the space, the glinting metal looked even more deadly against her skin.

The wind wasn't loud enough to mask Tom's whimpering. "I said be careful, Jake. Don't cut her."

The grit stung Jake's face when he stopped and looked up. "Do you want to do it?"

Tom shook his head.

Swallowing did nothing to ease Jake's sand coated throat or pounding pulse. The sharp weapon shook in his grip. What if he maimed her? Killed her? In the corner of his eye, Jake could see Tom bouncing on the spot like a child needing a piss. Turning on Tom again, he frowned hard at his friend. "Would you please stop that?"

"I just want you to be careful. Please don't cut her... or her hair."

"To be completely honest, mate, I don't give a shit about her hair. I'm sure she won't either when she realises her life has been a lie for the past three years. I'm more worried about her ear at the moment."

"Oh God. Please stay focused on what you're doing, Jake."

With his slim shoulders clamped to his neck, Jake gripped the handle of the knife until his knuckles were white. It tamed the wobble ever so slightly. "I will if you shut the fuck up."

"I hate what they've done to this world and the people in it." Jake looked up to see Tom tilt his head to one side as he looked at his wife. "She's a mess."

"Look, mate, I know this is hard for you, but we don't have the time to talk about it now. Are you ready?"

Tom nodded. "Yep."

Clenching his jaw, Jake pulled the blade up. It made light work of the first strap and didn't cut her. The Bots were coming now for sure. The second strap went just as easily. Jumping to his feet, Jake pointed at her. "You need to be quick, Tom. Are you sure you're up for this?"

Tom's eyes were glazed. His wobbling head barely nodded.

Running around behind her, Jake slid his hands under her fat shoulders; the rubble beneath her raking his skin. "Tom! Help me out, man."

Clarity cut through Tom's vacant expression. Rushing to Jake's side, he helped lift her.

Fire tore through Jake's biceps and his entire body shook. With both men grunting and moaning, they slowly raised Thalia from the ground.

Jake held her in place and tried to blink away the sweat stinging his eyes; each breath shallower than the last as he shook more vigorously. "Hurry up, Tom! The Bots will be here soon."

The only thing Jake saw move was Tom's Adam's apple. It bobbed on his long neck.

"Hurry up, for fuck's sake!" he bellowed at Tom.

The tall man moved around in front of her, grabbed the headset and froze again.

When Thalia slipped, Jake had to adjust his feet to hold her upright. Gravity was winning. "I can't hold her forever, man."

The glaze had returned to Tom's eyes as he stared at his wife's face.

An acrid smell smothered Jake; settling on the back of his throat, it tasted like stale sweat. When he looked down, he saw excrement leaking over her waistband. Several heaves flipped his skinny body. What little strength he had in his arms vanished. His legs went bandy. His stomach clamped.

"Do you need me to do it, Tom?" he managed to say as more shit belched out from Thalia—Rixon's synthesised sludge went through the gamers like water.

Tom shook his head.

"Well, bloody hurry up then." Jake slipped again. The woman rolled to the side and grit flew into his eyes but adrenaline helped him stabilise her. "If you don't hurry up, I swear I'm going to drop her. If I drop her, she ain't coming back up again."

Tears glistened on Tom's cheeks.

"On the count of three, yeah?" Jake said. He looked around. Still no Bots.

Tom didn't respond.

"One…"

The tall man came to life. "Am I doing the right thing, Jake? Will she be grateful for being freed from New Reality? Is a harsh truth better than a fake paradise?" His eyes widened. The effort of shouting turned his face the colour of beetroot. "*Will this fucking work?*"

Cramps held Jake's shoulders in a tough grip. "We can't turn back now. Two…"

Tom was hyperventilating.

"Three!"

"Argh!" Tom yanked the headset free.

Thalia's shrill scream pierced Jake's ears and all he wanted to do was drop her. It sounded like she was being skinned alive. The Bots must have heard that. The people in the tower probably heard that one too.

Tom held the headset in his hands as the food tube recoiled back inside and left a line of white syrup up his chest. Dropping it in disgust, Tom grabbed his wife's shoulders.

Jake stepped back and let Tom take the weight; his own limbs dangerously close to giving up. He stood next to his friend and rolled his tight shoulders while scanning for Bots. Any second now, and they would have to run.

Although Thalia had stopped screaming, her mouth was still flung wide and revealed yellow teeth set in her dark gums. The smell of dog shit filled the air. *Was that really her breath? Not even the wind could dispel it.* Jake thought and shuddered as he stepped back. He swallowed the hot saliva in his throat.

Reduced to a snapshot of suffering, she sat there. Greasy hair. A thick neck. Wide eyes. Her irises glaring a pained accusation. Frozen. Broken.

When she tilted to the side, Jake's stomach lurched. Watching Tom struggle to prevent her from falling, Jake wanted to help but he couldn't. She was sure to crush him if he tried.

Crack! Her temple hit a rock. Claret belched from the wound. Tom knelt down and brushed her hair from her face. Blood continued leaking out. Jake looked around again. Where were the Bots?

Putting his hand on Tom's bony shoulder, Jake shook his head. "There's nothing we can do. She's gone."

When Tom didn't respond, Jake leaned in close to hear him talking to her.

"We need to go, man. She's dead. There's nothing we can do. We need to get out of here before it's too late."

When Jake heard the mini helicopter blade approaching, tension snapped through his body and his bowels fell to his bollocks. It was already too late.

Chapter One

One year later.

"It's a trap."

Jake looked at the bloated corpse in the crater and then back to his tall friend. "You reckon?"

Tom nodded. "Definitely."

"What makes you say that? They haven't set traps for us before."

"No, but they probably thought we wouldn't last this long."

Following the line of Tom's gaze, Jake stared at the onyx tower in the far off distance. It was mostly hidden by dust clouds, but the red writing down its side glowed like a ruby in murky water. Each letter was at least seven stories tall, and although he couldn't read them from where he was, Jake knew what they spelled. The horizon was branded with the name of the world's new deity— RIXON. "So you still think they want us dead?"

"Absolutely. I think they would have wanted it to be from natural causes, but their patience must be wearing thin. We've lived without headsets for four years now— even the initial objectors put them on within the first year. We may be the only two still defying them."

Looking at the naked gamer at the bottom of the crater, Jake's eyes settled on the shiny glasses on his face. They looked brand new.

Pointing down the hill at the headset that had fallen off and was on its side next to gamer, Tom shrugged. "If it's not a trap, then why have they left that there? They're normally super-efficient at cleaning up after themselves, so why not this time?"

The grit in Jake's eyes burned so bad he wanted to claw them out. "Maybe you're right, maybe it's a trap. But that doesn't mean they want to kill us. Maybe they just want us to play New Reality." Scratching his beard, he blinked several times, his eyes streaming. "I need those sunglasses."

"Of course. We both do. That's why they've put them there."

Clenching his teeth, Jake glared at his friend. "Yeah, but I saw them first!"

Pulling his head back as if the words had dealt him a physical blow, Tom held his hands up. "Calm down, pal. I know you saw them first. All I'm saying is that you shouldn't go in there because you'll die. Come on, Jake, open your eyes. Can't you see what's happening?" Tom counted the points out on his fingers. "One, there's a dead gamer with something we need. It's the first dead gamer we've seen in four years—"

"But what about—"

Tom growled through clenched teeth. "It's the first dead gamer we've found lying around, all right?"

Biting his tongue, Jake watched Tom's face redden. They didn't need to talk about Thalia.

Clearing his throat, Tom continued, "Two, not only is it the first corpse we've seen, but it's the first pair of glasses we've found. Think about how many people used to wear glasses. Don't you think it's strange that we haven't found a single pair before now? And three, how are they even on his face? It's impossible to put a headset on without taking them off."

Looking down at the fat gamer, Jake suddenly realised just how blurry his vision was. "I want those glasses, Tom."

"Of course you do. They're banking on that. I'm sure the only thing that stopped them leaving a Christmas hamper with a pre-cooked turkey was the fact that they knew we'd share it. They had to leave a prize that we'd tear each other to pieces for. That's the sport of it."

The thought of roast turkey pulled at Jake's concave stomach, and the metallic taste of hunger lifted onto the back of his tongue. "So you're saying I shouldn't go for the glasses I found?"

"Jesus, Jake, you're not listening to me. I'm saying that neither of us should go and get them. We have no idea what they plan to do to us once we're in the crater, but I'd bet it ain't nice."

"They might only want to entice us into playing New Reality. But I don't want the headset. I want the glasses." After jabbing an angry finger at his friend, he said, "Besides, it's easy for *you* to say we should leave them, you have nothing to lose. Those glasses are rightfully mine."

Before Tom could reply, Jake added, "Maybe he died of natural causes and the headset fell away."

"Natural causes? I wouldn't call filling someone with so much sugary sludge they die from heart disease 'natural causes.' And, ignoring the fact that you can't wear a headset and glasses at the same time–like I just said–if he died on his own, why haven't they collected the headset? I've not known them to hang around in the past."

"Maybe he's only just died."

Tom raised his eyebrows. "Maybe."

"Don't patronise me, Tom."

"You make that hard. Besides, we're talking in circles and it's tiresome."

"So if they want us dead, why don't they send a Bot to take us out?"

"They don't want blood on their hands—at least not directly. If they had a reason to kill us, they could rebuild the world and convince themselves it isn't built on the death of millions. All the fat gamers die of heart disease and the nuisances like us die from tragic 'accidents.'" Tom threw air quotes with his fingers.

Jake's entire body leaned towards the crater. The dark glasses wedged on the bloated corpse's fat head were calling to him. "I saw those glasses first, so I'm taking them."

"You're going to risk your life for a pair of sunglasses?"

Jake looked at the crow's feet that radiated from Tom's bloodshot eyes. They spread halfway around his head. He looked at the flecks of blue that hinted at his once colourful irises. Years of dust storms had diluted them to nothing. "Yep. They ain't just sunglasses. They're sight! I don't want to be blind in a couple of years' time."

"Don't you remember what happened last time? With Thalia?" He couldn't say her name without his mouth buckling and his voice wavering.

The scar tissue ached on the back of Jake's triceps, aggravated by the memory. He looked at Tom. "I do… and I paid the price for it. I took a bullet for you so you could do what you had to do. I stood by you when all I wanted was to run."

The long man's tense frame sagged.

Lifting one of Tom's long and cold hands in both of his, Jake said, "All I'm asking you to do is keep a look out for me. You don't have to put yourself in the line of fire like I did; just warn me if a Bot's coming."

When Tom neither agreed nor disagreed, Jake patted him on the shoulder and said, "Thanks."

He then plunged into the crater.

###

Thrusting his arms out for balance, Jake rode the landscape as the debris slipped beneath his feet. The rush of rocks sounded like gushing water.

Something caught Jake's eyes, but he was traveling too fast to see what it was. It wasn't a Bot, of that he was sure. His breath escaped him; it must be *them*.

Hitting level ground, Jake fell to the floor. When his knees smashed down, a sharp pain ran from them, up his thighs, and into his stomach. Gasping, he took three deep breaths, scrambled to his feet, and moved on. No time to wait. Even if the Bots weren't coming, the things almost certainly were.

As he headed for the gamer, Jake turned to see Tom looking in the direction where he'd just seen movement. Had he seen them too? Would he say something if he had? He said he didn't believe they existed. Surely that was a lie. How could he not have heard them at night? How could he not have seen the shifting shadows? How could he not have felt them watching? He had to believe in them as much as Jake did; he was just too scared to admit it.

In Jake's mind, they were salivating, stinking human mutations that craved blood—horrors born of this toxic world. A shudder rattled through him. Whatever they were, they were getting braver and it wouldn't be long before they revealed themselves.

Maybe they took the corpses away. The gamer's died, the headsets fell off, and then they showed up to remove the body and feed on them. Gritting his teeth against the pain in his legs, Jake pushed forward. The glasses were his.

The ground shifted beneath his feet, sapping his strength with every stride. He moved as quickly as he could. Too fast and he'd break an ankle. Too slow and he'd lose his prize—maybe his life.

Although the crater acted as a wind block, he still had to dip his head to avoid being blinded by grit. Squinting as he looked up, he focused on the naked gamer's glasses. Lying there with the grey skin of a waxwork, the gamer was spread across the uneven terrain. The nipples on his flabby chest rested on each arm.

When Jake looked over his shoulder, Tom tapped an imaginary watch on his wrist.

Like he didn't know time was short. Idiot. As Jake dropped down next to the gamer, his raw joints screamed like they were filled with sand.

The stink of shit hit him and a slow heave rolled through his gut. All the gamers smelled the same when you got too close. Constant exposure to the gassy smell of decomposition had desensitised him to it but he didn't want to get so well acquainted with the smell of human excrement.

Looking around again, Jake saw nothing. *What are those things waiting for?*

When he tugged the glasses, they came free easily; almost as if they'd only just been placed there. Jake looked around again. The acrid stench of shit sent another heave through his stomach. He quickly stood up and stepped back

Jake was surprised when he put the glasses on and he could see through them clearly. Shouldn't they be scratched? Maybe Tom was wrong; maybe they'd been protected by the headset for the entire time.

Having worn a permanent squint for the past few years, Jake couldn't relax his face behind the protection of the lenses. That would take time.

With his eyes shielded, Jake saw farther into the storm than he'd ever managed to before; although it wasn't far enough to reveal anything new in his world. Imagining a Bot bursting through the clouds of dirt, Gatling guns trained on him, Jake pressed a hand to his heart in an attempt to slow down the sudden palpitations of fear.

But he hadn't done anything wrong. They had no reason to kill him. He had to remember that. They'd looted from gamers before and been fine. It was interfering with the headsets that Rixon got uptight about. The other things? He didn't know what pushed their buttons but just the thought of them made his stomach clench like a fist around a light bulb.

"Hurry up!" Tom called down, causing Jake to jump. His voice was both muffled by the wind and the tight scarf tied across his mouth.

Something moved in Jake's peripheral vision– something dark and languid. Then it was gone.

"Jake! For fuck's sake, man! Hurry the fuck up!"

Stepping towards his friend, Jake stopped again when something else caught his eye. Tom didn't swear often, but it wasn't often that Jake found a discarded headset. There was a white teardrop of synthesised sludge hanging from the food tube. Staring at it, pregnant with sustenance, Jake's arid mouth started to water and his dry tongue lifted involuntarily. He stopped himself from tasting it when Tom called again, "Jake!"

"Alright, alright. Keep your mane on, Seabiscuit."

Tom's face fell slack as if living up to his moniker. "Stop calling me that."

Jake presented his friend with the back of his middle finger before returning his attention to the headset.

"What are you doing, Jake?"

When Jake looked up, he saw that Tom had a metal bar in his right hand. What had he seen? Was it them? Would he admit it if it was? Glancing in the direction he expected the monsters to be, Jake still saw nothing.

The headset was the second one Jake had seen that wasn't attached to a gamer. He could crack it. How hard would it be to get the food tube working for them? That would shut Tom up.

The long man was still glaring at him, so Jake pretended to examine the gamer.

"He's not been dead long." Some flies flew out of the cadaver's mouth when he nudged his face with his foot. He swallowed and grit shifted in his throat like he had flies of his own. Jake continued, "I'd say he was in his forties."

Putting his foot on the big man's forehead, Jake rolled it from side to side. "He could do with shedding a few pounds, mind. The game really isn't good for your health." It hurt his throat to shout over the wind.

"He looks better than either of us, Jake. And we're probably younger than him."

Looking at his own body and then up at his friend; the pair of them seemed about as well cared for as prisoners of war. Jake accepted Tom's point with a shrug. "I'm sure he's only just died; that's why the headset's still here."

"It's a trap, Jake! Everything about this world is a bloody set up. A crater with a prize in it? Could it be any more inviting? Just hurry the fuck up!"

When Jake turned his full attention back to the headset, Tom's voice faded into the wind and Jake said, "Why do you think they still feel the need to brand everything?"

"Fucking hell, Jake, get away from the fucking headset before it's too fucking late!"

"I mean, it's not like the technology could belong to anyone else. They've won the corporate race; they have a monopoly on the world."

"They're reminding you who your master is. They're reminding you they're always watching. That you only exist with their permission," Tom paused before adding, "Maybe you should pay attention to *that*. Besides, do I need to remind you that we're still looking for Rory? I don't want anything to jeopardise that."

"Of course not, Tom." It had been over a year since they'd last seen Tom's son. The boy lay beside his mother and had already been playing New Reality for three years by then. All Tom wanted at the time was to stay with him, but after removing Thalia's headset, Rixon didn't want them anywhere near the boy. The Bots had shepherded them away for days; their Gatling guns the sharp teeth that nipped at their heels when they strayed too far off course. They'd been looking for him ever since.

Bending down, Jake peered into the headset. His right hand opened and closed; itching to grab the strap. The muscles in his weak arm buzzed with the desire to reach out.

"Don't, Jake."

Jake ignored him.

"Have you not seen what those Gatling guns do to the foxes and crows that accidentally touch one?"

Jake thought about the crow he'd recently seen explode from a barrage of bullets. It went up like a balloon filled with glitter.

When Jake knelt down, the rubble shifted by his feet and made the headset wobble. Adrenaline put a spring in his legs and he jumped back—to touch it was to die.

"Is the food tube malfunctioning, Jake? Is that what you're looking at?"

Jake shook his head.

"Damn it. Stop wasting our time then. You're putting both of us in danger. Leave it alone and hurry up!"

"There must be a way to hack this thing." Several burning coughs exploded from Jake's tight lungs.

"You and I both saw what happened the last time we tampered with a headset." Grinding his jaw, Tom waved a bony fist. "I swear; if you don't hurry up, then I'm off. You can fight a Rixon-Bot on your own. There's no way to hack a headset." Lifting a rock to make his point, he said, "You'd have better luck with this. You're hungry and deluded, now hurry up."

Holding his concave stomach, nausea sending a sharp pain through him as it gurgled in protest, Jake whispered to himself, "I'm not hungry. I'm starving."

"Listen Jake, even if you did manage to hack it, there's no way we'd be able to keep it," Tom pointed out. "Rixon would terminate us within seconds for stealing their property. All it needs is a tracking device to know where the headset is. It's not rocket science. Besides, they're always watching us anyway."

Suddenly Tom stopped talking and his jaw fell loose.

Before Jake could question him, he heard the sound.

Thwip, thwip, thwip, thwip, thwip.

It was a small helicopter blade.

Witnessing his own fear in Tom's panicked face; Jake looked back at the headset. Should he just take it and run?

His breath quickened. He searched around. Where was the Bot? Whipping around, he continued to look for it. He hadn't touched it. He hadn't done anything wrong. All of the muscles in his body locked tight. His pulse galloped. He hadn't touched it. He hadn't done anything wrong. He hadn't touched it. He hadn't done anything wrong.

Where was the Bot? What would it do to him? He hadn't done anything wrong. Please, *he hadn't done anything wrong.*

The noise grew louder.

***

Watching Jake and Tom was a break from the madness. Stepping away from the tornado of chaos and bloodshed, she sat observing the two. If sides were to be taken, she was on Jake's. Jake was right, the monsters were real. Running her tongue over her dry lips, she stared at Tom. He'd come to realise that soon enough.

Chapter Two

Holding his stomach as he laughed, Jake pointed at the mangy fox scratching itself. It was sat beneath a sheet of corrugated metal. Its whirring back leg spun like a propeller, flipping the sheet: *Thwip, thwip, thwip, thwip.*

"It's just a fox, Tom. Little shit." He covered his chest with his palm, his heavy heartbeat kicked against it. "I thought I was going to have a heart attack then. Jesus!"

Jake picked up a rock and launched it at the flea-bitten canid. Missing it, the rock sailed several metres wide and only managed to startle the animal. After the fox had run away, Jake looked up at Tom.

Tom pointed down at the ineffectual projectile and disappointedly said, "That's why we're starving."

Throwing his arms up, Jake replied, "I've not seen you do any better."

Tom's blank expression was made all the more barren considering his once brilliant blue eyes were now gunmetal grey. When he turned to look out over the wasteland, the wind made streamers of his raggedy clothes. Speaking with a sigh, he shook his head, "Please just hurry up, Jake. I'm leaving in one minute. I can't put my life in danger for you any longer. You've got what we came for."

As Jake began to walk away, he looked back one last time at the glossy headset. It shone against the battered surroundings. Holding his breath, Jake reached forward.

"Leave it alone, Jake." Tom tapped his wrist. "I'm gone in forty-five seconds."

Before Jake could protest, something else grabbed his attention. Staring at the small hill in front of him, he could hear a slow and deliberate scratch coming from the other side. Imagining a black diamond tough fingernail, Jake envisioned it moving over dry concrete towards them. Each stroke sent a shiver snaking down his spine.

Unable to control his shaking legs, Jake continued to stare; expecting something to appear. A hollow face. Blackened skin. A charred and forked tongue tasting the air, licking cracked lips. Sharp teeth that craved soft flesh. Goosebumps rose all over his body and he stepped back.

"Hurry up!"

Jake glanced over his shoulder and saw Tom's face slack with fear as he also stared in the direction of the sound. There was something there for sure.

Walking backwards in Tom's direction even more, Jake returned his focus to the hill. "What is it, Tom? What can you see?"

"Thirty seconds, Jake." There was a quiver in his voice that wasn't there before.

A lump of brick slipped beneath Jake's foot; his pulse spiked as his arms wind milled. Managing to stay upright, he gasped for breath. "Can you see them, Tom?"

"See who?"

Gulping an earthy mouthful of dust, Jake continued stepping back while thinking that Tom was the worst liar.

"You can, can't you?" Jake croaked out as the scratching got louder. "What do they look like? How many of them are there?"

"What are you talking about? You're imagining things, Jake. Just fucking hurry up. Jesus, how many times do I have to say it? I'm worried that a Rixon…"

Thwip, thwip, thwip, thwip.

No way was he falling for that again; Jake turned to look for the fox… but it was long gone

Rising up behind Tom like some monster from a lagoon, a large Rixon-Bot cast the tall man in shadow.

Cowering beneath it, Tom flinched as it flew past him.

It was in front of Jake in the blink of an eye. Jake swallowed back the need to cough as an itch burned in his gritty throat.

The metre-long machine hovered just centimetres away. It was black like the headset with RIXON embossed in blood red letters down its side. As it drew closer, the chill of its cold metal shell radiated from its heavy body. Jake shivered. His lungs tightened. Stars swam in his vision. His heart throbbed in his neck.

The machine's lens was about the size of a dinner plate and reflected everything back at Jake—his wide eyes, gaping mouth, and dilated pupils. It revealed nothing of the machine itself other than cold detachment. Jake's life wasn't important.

Swallowing twice in quick succession did nothing to ease his need to cough. Would it startle the machine? Could you startle a machine? The sudden sound could be perceived as a threat. He couldn't chance it.

The Bot remained still; the mini helicopter blade whirring to keep it stationary as the smell of oil filled the air. Jake's stuttered breath turned to condensation on the lens. Darkness shifted behind the glass as though a decision was being made. Thumb up or down? The shiny Gatling guns hung beneath it—level with Jake's soft stomach.

Breathe, Jake.

When the Bot flew backwards, Jake shook. The hot bullets would tear through him like needles through wet tissue. Jake closed his eyes and the sting of warm urine ran down his thigh.

Please make it quick.

Opening his eyes again, Jake saw the Bot fly at him. He ducked at the last moment and it sailed straight over his head. The gust of wind blew his hair from his face. Half an inch lower and… he couldn't think about it.

Spinning around as he stepped back, Jake tripped and fell onto a large lump of concrete. When Jake yelped as nauseating pain burned through his lower back, the machine spun to face him again.

Instead of attacking, the Rixon-Bot watched Jake but didn't move. Maybe it wasn't bothered; maybe Jake was right. He hadn't touched their property, so why would it want him?

The machine turned away again and hovered over the headset. A small hook extended from its underside, curled around one of the straps, and lifted it from the ground. The black helmet swayed beneath it in the wind.

Despite the very real threat to his life, Jake still wanted the headset.

As the Bot rose out of the crater, the headset was tossed and flipped by the elements. The Bot hovered for a second and then accelerated away; taking Rixon's property with it.

Jake released a long stream of air from his puffed cheeks before falling into a coughing fit.

After a minute or two, Jake looked up at his friend and laughed nervously. "Wow, I thought I was done for... Tom?"

Tom was staring over the brow of the hill where the scratching had been coming from. The skin on his previously white face had turned translucent.

When Jake tried to move, an acute agony stretched up his back, restricting his already tight lungs. Holding a hand out to his friend, he wheezed, "Tom! Help me out."

The tall man didn't move.

"Come on, Tom."

Then he heard the scratching again. Clicking nails; scuttling feet—there was more than one of them. The things had waited for Rixon to leave so they could claim the leftovers as theirs.

Forgetting his pain, Jake jumped up and scrambled to get away. He fell forwards onto the hill and started using both his arms and legs to gain purchase on the rubble to get out of the crater. The awkward movement threatened to crick his back and his limbs burned as the ground shifted.

The sound of feet chased him. *Clickety-click.*

Don't look around. Focus on Tom.

Slipping back down the hill, Jake kept his eyes up. *Don't look around. Focus on Tom.* It didn't help that Tom held his mouth wide in a silent scream as he fixated on what was approaching behind Jake.

Stars flashed in Jake's vision as he gasped to fill his burning lungs. The glasses did nothing to stop the streaming from his eyes that reduced Tom to a blur. The limp horror he still saw on his face only made Jake dig deeper and push on.

When Jake finally fell over the top of the hill, his pulse swelled in his eyeballs and sweat ran down his face. Seconds later, a sharp pain bit into his shoulder.

"Argh!" he growled and looked up to see that Tom had a hold of him.

"Don't look around," Tom said through gritted teeth. His eyes were wide. "Let's go."

The dusty air didn't seem capable of supplying enough oxygen for Jake's getaway, but Tom wasn't one to exaggerate. He'd have to cope. With nausea boiling in his guts, Jake followed on the heels of his departing friend.

The clickety-click behind them quieted down and as much as Jake wanted to turn around, he didn't. What mattered was that they weren't giving chase. Then Jake heard a wet squelching sound like pigs feeding.

That was why they never found any corpses.

***

She swallowed the thick lump of meat. It was bland. Salty.

Jake had escaped Rixon's wrath today. If it wasn't for Tom, he would have turned around and seen them. Would he have surrendered there and then? Would he have lost the strength in his legs and the will to survive? Would that have been the end?

The questions were pointless. She chewed the grey meat and watched those around her that were too preoccupied to notice Jake. That was good; Jake was hers.

Chapter Three

Moving at a quicker pace than usual, Jake slipped on a lump of rubble. A spike of panic gripped him and caused him to pause as he anticipated the crack of his ankle that never came. Jake stared into the oncoming wind with his eyes protected for the first time and could barely see his friend. As Tom disappeared into the dust storm ahead, Jake cupped his mouth and called after him, "Tom! Wait up, man."

The weather chewed his words up and spat them back in his face with a side helping of grit. Jake's cheeks burned from the sandblasting, despite the glasses enabling him to see better, but he kept his face up. To look down could mean losing his friend forever; the clouds already threatened to consume him completely.

With his heart beating like it was trying to bash free of his chest, Jake pushed on. In the past two years, they'd never been out of one another's sight and he wasn't going to let that happen now. He narrowed his eyes and kept his focus on Tom.

When Tom turned around again, Jake waved his arms in the air.

"Tom!" The shouting irritated his itchy throat. Resting his hands on his knees, he bent over double, gasping in between hacking coughs.

Coughing to the point where gritty phlegm lifted up his throat, Jake vomited a bitter mix of bile and mucus. He remained bent over and fought to catch his breath; his mouth stretched wide beneath the scarf covering it.

Every time he stood upright, another attack stopped him still. If he lost sight of Tom… he shook his head to banish the thought and continued trying to breathe.

By the time Jake had recovered, Tom was just a silhouette in the storm. Biting down on his lip, he pushed on, his lungs burning, his head spinning.

Having not stopped since leaving the crater, Jake's legs felt like they'd trebled in weight—every step threatened to sap what little energy he had left. Dizzy and nauseous, he reached his tolerance for looking into the wind, dropped his head and carried on.

The area was littered with evidence of a previously corporate monopolised society. Carrier bags were strewn amongst the wreckage; all of them had different logos but they all belonged to the same parent company.

A glance up showed him that Tom's outline was still there… just.

With grit clinging to the sweat dampening his forehead, Jake looked back down. Again his vision was filled with the excess of garbage. This time, he noticed the empty beverage cans. There was a variety of flavours and designs; also all owned by the same monopoly.

Presuming Tom was doing the same, Jake kept glancing back. It meant nothing that he couldn't hear their pursuers; the things following them existed in the shadows and only made their presence felt when they wanted to.

There was more evidence of their bygone society as he walked on—toys, books, old DVD's… all of them licensed by the same merchandising giant.

All Patrick Rixon had done with New Reality was to enter the consumer marketplace with the best product. The free market economy allowed the strongest to survive and monopolise. At just twenty-three, the German did what his fellow countryman of over a century and a half ago had tried to do—he'd taken over the world.

Sweat ran into Jake's eyes when he looked up. Blinking several times, he returned his attention to Tom. There was no sign of him slowing down. He must be exhausted.

Jake tripped and the air left his lungs.

Pain tore into his right shin seconds later and spread through his leg. Rolling onto his back, the jagged ground spiky against his spine, Jake pulled his knees to his chest. Rubbing the point of impact like he was trying to set his leg on fire helped but only a little.

Jake jumped when he looked up and saw a sharp steel blade close to his face. Protruding from the ground like a trap, he'd missed it by mere centimetres. The thought of landing on it made his already weak body weaker. How were they still alive in this place?

Shaking the thought away, Jake lifted his head and looked for Tom. He still hadn't stopped.

When Tom finally looked back again Jake lifted his upper body to wave his arms in the air and called in a weak voice, "Tom!"

He then collapsed from the effort and the hard impact caused him to bite down on his tongue. The metallic taste of his own blood ran down his phlegmy throat as Jake watched Tom turn back around and continue to march away.

If Jake didn't get to his feet now, then he'd surely lose him forever.

With sweat itching beneath his clothes, he pushed himself up on his good leg. The injured one pulsed and when he put light pressure on it, his heart fluttered. He expected it to fold beneath him but it didn't. Pushing down harder hurt more, yet it wasn't broken and there wasn't time to hang around. Setting off after Tom, Jake now moved with a heavy limp.

If Jake had any chance of catching up with his friend, Tom would have to slow down. Shouting so loud that he shook, Jake called, "Tom! I'm sorry, man. I thought we'd be okay for a while."

Tom didn't respond.

"Tom, come on, man, wait up!"

When Tom looked over his shoulder again, Jake shouted, "Come on, Tom! Hear me out, mate."

He slowed down to a stop and when Jake hobbled close enough, he saw the deep frown on his friend's face.

Looking him up and down, Tom shielded his eyes as he rubbed both temples with the thumb and index finger of one hand. "What have you done to yourself?"

Taking several steps closer, Jake stopped and rested his hands on his knees. His head spiralled as he pulled air into his oxygen starved lungs.

After a couple of minutes, Tom made a point of looking at an imaginary watch and then behind them in the direction of the things.

"Sorry, man," Jake wheezed. Holding up his index finger, he added, "Let me get my breath back... one more minute."

While looking past his friend again, Tom spoke in a dry voice, "Been a day for waiting, hasn't it?"

Ignoring the snarky comment, Jake kept his focus on his breathing.

After taking his full minute and then some, Jake stood upright and interlocked his fingers behind his head. A sharp headache throbbed behind his stinging eyes. The saliva in his parched mouth had turned to a thick and bitter paste.

"I'm sorry, man." Drawing another deep breath, he winced at the burn in his lungs. "I really am."

Watching Tom's face twist as he pulled a heavy gulp, Jake could only assume the lack of liquid was affecting him in a similar way. When Tom spoke, his voice came out in a croak.

"You never listen to me. Next time, I'm leaving you on your own." He scratched his face, sharp and hard, and then squinted as he looked behind Jake again.

Jake twisted to see what his friend was looking at, then turned back around and studied his face. "What did you see over the hill?"

Dropping his eyes, Tom shook his head. "Nothing; I didn't see anything. I just wanted you to hurry up."

"Then why did you tell me to not look behind?"

Looking beyond Jake yet again, Tom bounced on the spot. "Why did you fuck about so much?"

"What are we running from, Tom?" Jake pried, unwilling to drop it.

"What are you talking about?" Tom's grey eyes were wildly unsettled.

"If there was nothing to see behind earlier," Jake asked, "then why did you stop me looking? Why are we running?"

"I'm not running." Jabbing a long finger at Jake, Tom sneered. "I just want to be away from you."

"That's not it, Tom. You saw them, didn't you? What did they look like?"

"Stop talking rubbish. I didn't see anything."

When Jake didn't reply, Tom looked away and ground his jaw. After a few seconds, he looked back, his gaunt face locked tight. "Do you appreciate how hard it was for me to stand watch while I worried about you being killed?

36

You were so vulnerable in that bloody crater, and you wouldn't listen to me."

The scar tissue burned in Jake's triceps. It had been just over a year, and he could feel the wound as if it were still healing. At the time, it felt like the Bot had taken his arm clean off. Staring straight at his friend, he raised an eyebrow. "I know exactly how it feels, Tom."

When Tom's harsh posture sank, Jake's heart ached. He'd pushed it too far. "I'm sorry, man."

Tom didn't respond.

"I'm sorry, I shouldn't have gone there." When would he learn to think before he spoke? Talking about Thalia was out of order.

Tom stared straight through him with glazed eyes as if he hadn't spoken.

Grabbing his glasses, Jake paused before removing them and handing them to Tom. Squinting, he shielded his eyes with his free hand. "Here, have these. I'm sorry."

After clearing his throat, Tom brushed loose strands of his hair away from his forehead. He kept his hair pulled back in a severe ponytail, but it was no match for the strong winds. He looked at the glasses through tear-filled eyes, began to reach for them, and then paused. Crow's feet stretched across his temples as his face showed his distain. "I don't want your stupid glasses."

He sighed deeply again and then looked across at the menacing obelisk sky-scraper on the horizon. Other than the dusty sun, which they saw infrequently, it was the only thing on the skyline.

"Are you sure?" Jake said, as he lifted the glasses towards his friend.

His question was answered with a scowl.

The relief was instant when Jake slipped the glasses back on. Allowing his weeping eyes to clear the grit themselves, Jake ignored the burn as much as he could and followed Tom's line of sight over to the dark tower. Running down its spine, blurred on the horizon, it read RIXON. An exact replica of the tower dominated every city.

"I can't believe our only landmark is that phallic symbol of oppression," Jake said. "Look at it; it's penetrating the clouds like they're the world's arsehole. Quite fitting really…" He then threw it the bird.

It was nice to see Tom's eyes brighten and the scarf across his mouth lift as if he were smiling before he said, "Someone probably saw that. I'd imagine those arseholes controlling our lives love that kind of reaction. It shows they're winning."

"You really think the rich have retreated into the towers and our lives are entertainment for them?"

"Of course, I do! It may have looked like Rixon crushed all of the other companies, but the previous corporations' grip on the world was too firm—there's no way they simply vanished. Those companies set the rules, not Rixon. He only succeeded with their permission. For all we know, Patrick Rixon's just a front for them. I guarantee you that the fat cats from before are the ones waiting in the towers now." Turning to look at Jake, he raised his eyebrows and continued, "As for us as entertainment? What else are they going to do while they wait for everyone to die?"

Whether Tom was right or not, living in such a heightened state of paranoia wasn't for Jake. Searching their surroundings, he shook his head. "I can barely remember the city now. I try to imagine where the Cube Building once was... the University Clock Tower... the Alpha Tower."

"It's hard to remember Birmingham not looking like this, isn't it?" Scanning the wasteland, Tom wrinkled his nose. "Not stinking of death and decay."

Having got so used to the stench, it was only when it was pointed out to him that Jake could smell the decomposing gases.

Looking up, Jake watched the broiling clouds. Grey and heavy, they looked like they contained churning rocks that would rain down oblivion. "I couldn't quite believe what I was seeing when they levelled the city."

Tom didn't reply.

"The controlled explosions lasted for... what... about a week? I didn't get much sleep during that time. I got that much dust on my lungs that I don't feel like I've been able to breathe properly since."

Shaking his head, Tom said, "It was a crazy week. It was quite amazing to see how the Bots cleared the gamers out of a building, levelled it, and then put them back on the rubble. Their efficiency was impressive."

"They were designed by a German. What do you expect?"

The rag on Tom's face jumped away as a forced laugh shot from his mouth.

"It was a good idea of yours to hide by the Rixon Tower, Tom. There was no way they were blowing up their penis of corporate domination."

At first Tom didn't reply. Instead, he stared at the tower before finally sighing. "Sometimes I wonder if it was. We should have just let a building collapse on us; that would have been a hell of a lot easier."

Throwing another glance back in the direction they'd come from, Tom looked back at the tower.

"You don't…" Jake fell into a coughing fit. Once he'd recovered, he lifted the scarf covering his mouth and spat out a metallic-tasting bilious lump of phlegm before he continued, "…mean that."

Tears welled in his eyes as Tom said in a monotone, "I do. If I'd have known what we were going to do Thalia…" A frown dipped on his brow.

Without another word, Jake hobbled over to his friend and put an arm over his bony shoulder. The two of them stared at the tower.

###

After about five minutes of standing with his arm around Tom, Jake could feel the tingle of an impending cramp in

40

his shoulder. Unwrapping himself from his tall friend, he patted him on the back. "Come on, man, let's go."

Tears streamed from Tom's wide eyes as he stared into the distance, unblinking, even in the dust storm.

Clicking his fingers, Jake said, "Tom, come on, we've got to get moving."

When there was still no response, the only thing Jake could think of to say to get Tom's attention was, "What if they're still following us?"

Tom's eyes snapped even wider and he jerked his head round to stare in the direction they'd come from.

Moving closer to his friend, Jake spoke softly. "Why don't you tell me what they look like?"

Silence.

"Okay, mate, fair enough. We need to get moving though."

When the tall man still didn't reply, Jake began hobbling off on his still sore leg.

He stopped almost instantly when Tom said, "I can't believe that it was only four years ago when we were caught up in the rat race like every other mug." He chuckled humourlessly. "Do you remember the advertisements? They were everywhere."

Seeing his friend falling into a depressive spiral, Jake stepped away from him. "Come on, we need to keep walking. Thinking about the past isn't going to help anyone."

Wobbling under the force of nature, Tom imitated the gruff American voice selling the product that would change their world forever. He sounded like a voiceover for a Hollywood action movie trailer. *"Five dimensions is the future of entertainment. Now you can taste, touch, and smell what you're seeing and hearing. Rixon will give you the experience of your life. If you can think it, you can live it."* Shaking his head, he snorted a laugh. "It seemed so bizarre, like something you'd see in a movie. I never thought entertainment would be able to respond to your subconscious and give you everything you desired."

The bruise on Jake's shin throbbed as he set off again knowing Tom would follow. Two pairs of eyes were better than one and Tom, more than anything, was driven by the need to find his son.

***

She watched Jake walk away and then looked at his temperamental friend. Why did Jake even put up with him? All he did was drag him down with his depressing quest to find his son. There was so much out there for Jake if only he could cast his friend aside.

Not much time had passed since she'd started watching the pair, but she already knew her wishes were pointless. Loyal to a fault, Jake would keep Tom around regardless of the damage to himself.

Looking around at her brothers and sisters, all of them driven by a similar purpose and staring with obsessive intent, she let the tension slide from her shoulders. She couldn't control the situation. The only power she had was intervention, and it was far too early for that.

42

Chapter Four

After running his tongue around his frothy mouth, Jake swallowed his stale saliva. It did nothing to clear the gritty lump nestling in his throat and tasted like he'd fallen asleep halfway through eating a biscuit. Finding just enough liquid to survive, most of it being sugary drinks of one sort or another meant the bilious blockage never cleared; no matter how many times he swallowed.

He looked down and lifted his glasses while his voice rasped, "Oh, my."

Dropping into a hunch, both of his kneecaps popped as he reached out a weak arm. He feared that his hand would pass through the mirage that had made him instantly forget his discomfort.

However, when he touched the plastic wrapping, it crunched like plastic should. When he tried to lift the object, it was heavy like he'd have expected. Wobbling it, he watched the liquid swill around in the six large bottles. Jumping up so quickly his head spun, he called out, "Tom! Over here!"

The tall man was about twenty metres behind, still sulking about the incident with Jake and the dead gamer. It would have been nice to have him by his side like they had been for the past few years, but anything was better than losing sight of him. He turned his attention back to the bottles of water.

"Tom! I'm being serious, man. You've got to see this."

Stopping again, Tom looked up but didn't say anything. He then dipped his head into the wind and continued his slow march.

"I've found water, Tom!"

Tom snapped his head up and Jake could see he was confused.

"There's water here!"

Despite the distance and the dust, Jake could see the doubt in Tom's hunched body. Jake wouldn't want to get his hopes up either. He dropped back down and dug a bony finger into the plastic wrapping. Initially, he didn't know which would give first, his weak finger or the plastic, but he finally burst through the cellophane. Grabbing the neck of one of the bottles, he wobbled it to get it out, the containers creaking as they rubbed against one another.

Once it was free from the other five, he held it up in the air. The weight of the unopened two-litre bottle made his arm shake.

"Look, Tom. *Water!*"

Watching Tom's eyes widen and his mouth fall loose, Jake stood, smiling as his friend trebled his pace.

When he caught up, Jake handed it to him. "Can you believe it? It feels like weeks since we've had any."

"That's because it has been; two to be precise." After twisting the lid free, Tom added, "Since we've had water anyway."

With shaking hands, Jake pulled another bottle from the pack. The adrenaline rushing through him made removing the lid difficult. Taking deep breaths, he tried to calm down.

Finally, the lid came free and slipped from Jake's grip. The wind caught it, and it fell away from him, skipping over the rugged landscape like a flat stone over still water. Shrugging, Jake lifted the bottle to his lips and a couple of trickles of the cool liquid slid across his chin, down his neck, and under his collar. Jake shuddered as it ran a cold line down his chest.

The fresh water spread through his mouth, hydrating every crevice. His body was so thirsty that the first mouthful was practically gone before it reached his sticky throat.

Just as Jake upended the bottle for a second swig, Tom said, "Stop!"

Looking first into the upturned bottle and then lowering it, Jake licked his cracked, wet lips. "Why?"

"If you drink too fast, you'll give yourself a bad stomach."

"If I don't drink fast, I'll die."

"Don't be dramatic, Jake. You won't die; we've only been a day without liquid."

"But Coke hardly counts."

"It's had to."

Taking a small sip, Jake swallowed and threw his friend a facetious grin. "Better?"

Sneering, Tom shook his head and looked down at their prize. "Why are the bottles here?"

"Not this again."

Tom looked back at Jake. "Come on; don't tell me you think this is a coincidence." Glancing at the tower, he continued, "They're watching us. They've put this here for a reason."

A tingling sensation gripped Jake's back as if he could feel the surveillance they were under. Why did Tom always have to remind him that they were being watched? "Maybe they want us to have a drink."

"No, it's more than that. They don't give anything without taking something away." His eyes narrowed. "This is all a part of their sick game."

"Or maybe they just want to give us a drink?" Despite trying to assert his opinion, Jake could hear the ring of uncertainty in his own voice.

"You know there's more to it than that, Jake. You know as much as I do that they like to fuck with us."

Jake took another swig. "Well, whatever the reason, we should enjoy it while it lasts." Just before Tom could reply, Jake added, "Besides, if they want everyone dead so they can rebuild, why did they take all of the gamers out of the buildings before they levelled the city?"

Tom lifted his shoulders in a high shrug. "Dunno. Maybe the headsets are too valuable to destroy."

"Then why don't they just rip them off? We already know what that does to…" Jake snapped his hand over his mouth.

Glaring at Jake, Tom paused for a few seconds before clearing his throat. Desperation turned his voice reedy. "There has to be a way to remove the headsets without killing the gamers."

"Of course," Jake agreed. "Totally. I'm sure there's a way." The lie heated his face and he hoped Tom didn't notice. After all, they had to try and get a headset off Rory. "But my point still stands. If they want the gamers to die, why do they keep them alive? It doesn't make sense."

"Conscience, maybe?" Tom shrugged again. "Maybe they think letting the gamers die without their direct interference means they didn't do it. That would allow them to rebuild without guilt. It's amazing what lies people tell themselves to get through the day."

Watching his wide-eyed friend scan their surroundings as he spoke sent jitters through Jake. "Your paranoia's getting to me."

"It'll do you good. You need to be more alert."

Jake raised an eyebrow and laughed. "I think you're alert enough for the both of us."

He then lifted the bottle to his lips again, careful not to spill any this time, and waited for Tom's retort. That was when he heard it– a deep creaking like an old ship that was about to tear in half. It was so loud it shook the ground beneath them. When he looked at Tom, his pulse flipped into overdrive. His tall friend was staring back in the direction they'd just come from.

When Tom looked back at him, his grey eyes wild, his body shaking, Jake said, "What the fuck was that?"

***

As she watched, she ran her tongue across her teeth to liberate some of the fleshy fibres stuck between them. They'd finished their feast. The food had run out quickly. The pair best start running.

Chapter Five

Jake looked down at the four unopened bottles of water before he looked back up at the departing Tom and said with disbelief, "What are you doing, man? We can't leave this here."

Without breaking stride or turning around, Tom shouted, "We've got to go. Come on!"

"Tom!"

A scuttling sound like rushing water was gaining on them. This was more than a landslide, it sounded like an approaching army. Jake looked down at the bottles again.

Swallowing another mouthful of water, the stale phlegm on the back of his throat all but disappearing, Jake looked in the direction they'd come from. When he saw the cloud of dust in the distance, this time kicking up from the ground rather than riding the wind, goose bumps spread over his body. Running a hand through his hair, he tapped at his half-drunk bottle and then looked across at Tom and saw he wasn't slowing down.

Bouncing on the spot, Jake looked at the loose cellophane flapping in the wind around the four remaining bottles—the dust cloud was getting closer.

"Fuck it," he said and dropped the bottle in his hand. Water spurted from the open top when it hit the ground and Jake watched the precious fluid soak into a breeze block. The waste tore at his heart, but what could he do? Picking up a sealed bottle—one being all he could carry comfortably—Jake set off after his friend.

"Tom, wait up, man!"

Whether Tom heard him or not was unclear, but he wasn't stopping. Focusing all of his attention on Tom's long back, Jake gave chase. After only a few steps, the bruise on his shin ached and the recently consumed water swilled in his empty stomach.

Dragging shallow breaths into his tight lungs, Jake released a series of burps without slowing his pace.

When he caught up with Tom, he vomited a shot of the tasteless water into his mouth. He quickly swallowed the warm liquid back down again then spoke between breaths. "What... did you... see coming out of the... crater?"

Although Tom looked straight at him, his sharp grey eyes clearer than they had been in weeks, he didn't reply.

"Just tell me what you saw, man."

"What are you talking about, Jake?"

"Come on, you saw something."

Tom frowned. "I didn't see anything."

When he dropped his head and picked up his pace, Jake grabbed Tom's skinny shoulder and spun him around. "Wait!"

Although Tom stopped, his attention was behind them. "Why are you stopping me?"

"If there's nothing following us, then what are you looking at and why are we running?"

Tom just shook his head and stayed silent. Keeping a hold of his friend's shoulder, Jake stepped up onto a large rock. It wobbled beneath his feet.

"What are you doing?" Tom asked.

"Trying to get a better view."

"So there's no grit up there then?"

Staring at the large dust cloud on the horizon, which was no clearer from his elevated position, Jake threw Tom a tight smile. "All right, smartarse. It was worth a try at least."

"Was it? Why?" Tom asked sarcastically.

"Okay, it wasn't worth a try." When Jake stepped down, the jolt of landing on the ground sent bolts of electric pain up his shin. "Being two feet higher off the ground did nothing to help me see better. Happy?"

Shaking his long head, Tom frowned. "Not really. I'd much rather be able to see what was going on."

Folding his arms across his chest, Jake scowled at Tom. "Like you haven't seen them already…"

Tom stared at him for a moment and then, shaking his head, he walked off again.

Despite the near-deafening wind, Jake heard a low boom in the distance. It sounded like mortar fire. Running with a limp, he caught up with Tom again. Eyes wide and his breath short, he said, "Tell me you heard that."

Tom continued walking.

Jake had to skip every three paces to keep up. The effort put more strain on his already tight lungs and the water continued to swill in his guts. Every trip and stumble ignited the fire in his shin but there was no way he was losing Tom. Not now. Not ever.

It was Tom who spoke first this time. "You're imagining things, Jake. It's probably just another landslide."

"A landslide? A landslide doesn't bloody chase you!"

"It does if you're unlucky."

Looking behind, the cloud of dust closer than before, Jake said, "We're going uphill, Tom."

Tom shrugged and continued walking.

"You know exactly what's following us. You've bloody seen it."

The accusation was met with silence.

Another loud bang went off behind them, and Jake's stomach twisted. When he saw Tom's wide eyes, he pointed at him. "See, you heard it that time. I know you did."

Tom didn't reply.

"So, if there's nothing following us," he caught his breath, "what the fuck was that noise?"

Bang!

Jake's heartbeat ran away with him. "What is it, Tom?"

Bang!

The ground shook like it had a few minutes previously. Jake's throat became impossibly dry from fear and he desperately wanted to stop to drink, but Tom was moving faster than ever.

Bang!

The ground shook to the point where both of them had to steady themselves. "It's just the shifting landscape, is it?"

Tom's mouth hung loose, and a frown wrinkled his brow.

Bang!

Bang!

The last bang nearly took Jake off his feet.

Finding his voice, Tom said, "Faster! We need to move faster."

Bang!

Bang!

Bang!

Gritting his teeth against the pain in his leg, Jake sped up, overtook his friend, and somehow arrived at the bottom of the next hill first.

Bang!

The noise nipped at their ankles and was now accompanied by the skittering of a thousand spindly legs. It was like being chased by an army of giant spiders. Jake imagined a carpet of them coming over the hill, smothering him until he couldn't breathe. Gasping for air,

Jake's knees weakened and the next rock he stepped on shifted out from under his foot. He landed with a thump as the air was knocked out of his lungs.

Bang!

When Tom approached, Jake looked up from his crumpled position, paralysed with fear and exhaustion.

Looking down at Jake, Tom shook his head and carried on up the hill.

Jake looked back in the direction of the sound.

Bang!

"Tom! Tom! Help me! *Tom!*"

Turning to look up the hill, Jake watched the tall man reach the top, stare back at him for a second, and then disappear over the peak.

***

Grinding her jaw, she watched on. The dust on the wind was particularly thick today, but she still saw everything. Why did Tom just leave him? The friend that had given up the past few years of his life to search for his son—not to mention, his only friend left in the world—and he'd left him.

Shaking her head, she looked at Jake all alone on the floor; crumpled as he lay there and vulnerable to what was coming over the hill towards him.

Chapter Six

Staring at the space his friend had occupied seconds before and seeing only the haze of blowing sand, Jake shouted, "Tom, help me!"

How far away was he? Could he even hear him now?

Bang!

The ground shook again, and Jake grabbed onto a rock next to him. "Tom!"

The scuttling sound came forward in a wave. Any second and the things would burst through the dust cloud. Every atom of Jake's being wanted to run, but his impotent body wouldn't respond. Without Tom he was fucked; all he could do was wait. Tiny pops of grit hit the lenses on his glasses as he searched the storm. Holding onto his bottle of water as if it would offer him salvation, he remained alert and waited, his mouth dry, his body shaking.

The sound surrounded him, the wash of noise now in front and behind. Looking back up the hill, he shouted for Tom again. His heart sank; Tom was long gone.

There was still nothing to be seen but the ground rumbled harder than before. Having ignored the thought up until now, Jake found it impossible to push it from his mind—they were beneath him. Was that even possible? How could they move so quickly through the rubble?

Using his good leg, Jake pushed himself up the hill. The ground slipped and he barely moved. Pushing harder did nothing but shove the rocks and rubble away from him quicker. All his flapping did was remind the things chasing him that he was a warm meal in a world where everything was served cold.

When the ground rumbled again, Jake looked up the hill. His heart skipped. Stood at the top, fogged by the clouds of dust, was the silhouette of his tall friend. His eyes burned and tears streamed down his face. The already fuzzy world became large splurges of watercolour. Jake stretched his arm up. "Help me, please."

The tall man descended the slippery landscape, his arms thrust out to the sides for balance as he skidded down it.

He stopped when a deep yawn that sounded like a moaning whale groaned around them and caused the surrounding rocks to bounce with the vibrations.

Dust and dirt suddenly exploded from the ground between them. For the second time in as many minutes, Tom was lost to him. The deep yawning sounded again and the ground rocked.

When the dust settled, there was a crevice at least three metres wide between them.

Gritting his teeth, Jake got to his feet and hobbled towards his friend. He stopped at the edge of the fissure and looked down into it. It was too dark to see anything clearly; all he could make out was a river of perpetual black movement. He looked back at Tom. "Help me, man."

Shaking his head, Tom looked down at the undulating swarm in the ravine; his skin was pale when he looked back up. Searching the area around him, Tom shook his head again and took several steps back.

"Tom, where are you going?"

Tom pulled his hair away from his forehead, and then looked at his friend. Turning his attention to their surroundings, he picked up an electric flex and walked close to the edge of the gap. "Here, catch this."

Tom threw one end towards him but when he reached out to grab it, Jake looked down and his head spun. The cable slipped through his grip and Tom had to reel it in for a second throw.

Jake caught it this time. It was thin. Could it even hold his weight? "What are you going to do with this?"

Tom didn't reply. He simply stared.

"You don't know, do you?"

"No, I do. I was thinking—" The ground shook again, and Tom's eyes spread wide. Looking down, his feet not even a metre from the edge, Tom winced. "I'm sorry, Jake. I'm so sorry."

Standing with the limp cable in his hands, Jake watched Tom's back as he ascended the hill again. "Tom! Wait up, Tom. Help me, man. Tom!"

The ground shook. Swallowing the grit in his dry mouth, dizzy from the thick pulse crushing his skull, Jake searched for something—anything—of use. Unless he was going to throw rubble at whatever was beneath them, he was shit out of luck.

Thoom!

A hole as deep as the one he was staring into but twenty times wider opened up behind him. A mushroom cloud of dirt filled the sky. As the hole stretched, the debris in the surrounding area was drawn towards it and a whirlpool of rubble and masonry was sucked into the abyss. The entire landscape was changing before his eyes.

Turning in quick circles, hoping that a second look would reveal something that would help him, he caught movement out of the corner of his eye.

At first it looked like a long scaffolding board was wobbling in the strong wind. A couple of seconds later, Tom, red-faced and sweating, appeared over the hill. He slid down the slippery slope again and let the board fall across the gap; the end of it crashed to the ground centimetres from Jake's toes.

When Jake looked down at it, Tom shouted, "Hurry up! You don't have the time to think about it."

The black hole behind Jake continued to suck the landscape into it. Focusing instead on the narrow board, Jake watched it hop and jump with the vibrations. As he stepped forwards, another quake shook the ground.

The kneecap on his good leg took the brunt of the impact when he fell onto a jagged brick. The searing pain crippled his thigh even before the rest of his body landed.

Looking up at Tom, he shook his head and cried out, "I can't do it, man! I can't fucking do it!"

***

What could Tom really do to help? He was useless at best. All he'd done was drag Jake down and keep him in the ruined city. He was just prolonging the agony. There was no way Jake could cross the gap. He could barely stand, let alone walk that plank.

Chapter Seven

Staring at Tom on the other side of the gorge, Jake waved him away. "Go without me. I can't walk."

Tom looked at Jake for a moment and considered his options before he nodded and turned his back. After one step, he stomped his foot and spun back around. "Fuck it!"

"Just go. There's nothing you can do to save me."

"Fuck it!"

"Go!"

"Fuck it!"

"Stop saying that!"

Tom walked up to the edge of the plank and briefly looked down. His eyes snapped back up again and his cheeks puffed as he exhaled.

"What are you doing, Tom? Just bloody go already."

Tom closed his eyes and took several deep breaths. He then reopened them and placed a shaking foot on the plank.

Gulping dusty air, Jake choked out, "What are you doing?"

Staring at Jake, Tom said, "Will you please shut up? I'm concentrating."

Biting down on his bottom lip, Jake watched on in silence.

When Tom fully stepped onto the plank, it was hard to tell if the wobble was coming from the plank, the wind, or Tom's trembling body. Whatever the cause, the effect was horrific. There was no way Tom would make it across without falling to his death. Why was he even coming over? What did he plan to do once he'd crossed the gap?

As he reached the middle of the plank, Tom swayed in the strong wind. Burying his mouth and nose into praying hands, he closed his eyes and froze in place.

Watching his friend, panic stole Jake's breath.

The wind had picked up to the point where the tendrils of Tom's clothes were being blown sideways away from him.

The grit stung as it sandblasted the side of Jake's face. Rubbing his kneecap to soothe the burn, Jake gasped as Tom stepped forwards again, the board looking more unstable than ever.

Two quick strides and Tom jumped clear of the plank. The long lump of wood hopped several times, and Jake expected it to fall into the hole.

Landing on the rubble, Tom rested his hands on his knees and expelled a long breath. "Fuck."

After a moment's silence, Jake said, "So what are we going to do now?"

"We're going to cross back over."

Jake shook his head. "There's no way I'm crossing over that. No fucking way."

Looking at the dry whirlpool behind them as it chewed up the land like a giant waste disposal unit, Tom said, "It's getting bigger. If we don't cross this plank, we'll die. That's all there is to it."

"But I can't walk."

"Crawl then."

Staring at his friend, Jake didn't move.

"Hurry up, Jake. I didn't just risk my life for you to bottle it."

"But I can't do it."

Shaking his fist at him, Tom clenched his jaw and shoved Jake forwards with his foot. "You have to! I've just risked my fucking life for you!"

When Jake didn't move, Tom shoved him again, his entire body shifting closer to the edge. "Now get moving, you stupid bastard!"

Kneeling on his damaged knee, Jake's stomach contorted and he had to fight to stop himself vomiting. It felt like the patella had fractured in several places and every ounce of applied pressure crushed it like an eggshell. He turned around to look up at Tom and was met with a stony glare.

Jake shuffled forward and placed his water bottle in front of him before gripping either side of the rough wooden plank.

"Hurry up, Jake."

Feeling Tom's nudging foot against his bottom, Jake moved forward, placed his bottle farther ahead, and then moved forward again. Every time he put pressure on his knee, it sent electric pain through his groin and kidneys.

Jake became more aware of his surroundings with each movement forward— more specifically, the height of the drop. With each shuffle forward, the wobble in the board became more exaggerated and Jake realised that he couldn't turn back even if he wanted to.

Once he was halfway across, Jake froze as the wind battered his right side and threatened to capsize the plank. Gripping onto the board, he remained still and watched his water get blown over the edge. The full bottle spun into the darkness below and bounced off the moving carpet of black beneath them.

What sounded like a thousand high-pitched whistling screams shot out of the chasm. Had they mistaken the bottle for fresh meat? The mass below churned and twisted but eventually the sound died down.

When Jake felt Tom step onto the plank behind him, he looked around. "What are you doing, man?"

"Crossing. What does it look like?"

Another quake ran through the ground and debris fell into the abyss—one more shake like that and the plank was following it. Jake sped up.

The long board sagged and bounced with both of them on it and Jake's heart beat in his neck.

With less than a metre to go, the ground shook again. The end they were heading for slipped farther. Ignoring the pain in both of his legs, Jake pushed on. Gritting his teeth and grunting through the discomfort, he reached out to the rough rubble on the other side. Seconds later he was off the board and scrambling up the hill but Tom was still crossing.

Another heavy rumble made Tom freeze for the slightest moment, so Jake called, "Come on, man! Keep moving!"

As Tom took his next step forward, the ground shook again. At first, the board stayed in place... then Jake noticed the brick it was resting on. Dirt and debris was slipping past it, flowing like water around a rock. It didn't look like it would hold for long.

Glancing up at Tom, he saw the tall man's eyes focus on it. Looking back down at the brick, Jake held his breath as it started to shift.

Everything happened in slow motion. The brick moved again... then again.

Jake's mouth hung open and he gasped.

The brick slipped free.

***

She held her breath as she watched the plank slip; if Tom fell, then Jake would be rid of him. The tall man held him back and if Jake had any chance of avoiding his fate, Tom would have to go.

As long as he was friends with Tom, Jake would stay in this godforsaken city. As long as he stayed in the city, he was her responsibility. The longer he was her responsibility, the more likely it would be that she'd have to kill him.

Staring on with unblinking eyes, she watched the plank slip farther. There was no way Tom was walking away from this.

Chapter Eight

Jake reached towards his friend as the plank slid. "No!"

Like he had on the way over, Tom took two long strides and leaped. The second he jumped, the long plank slipped into the chasm.

At first, Jake thought the gap was too wide, but with the wind at his back, Tom seemed to fly. Rolling over to the side, the jagged landscape jabbing his body, Jake scrambled out of the way as Tom landed on the rubble beside him.

Tom remained crouched and panted for a few seconds before standing up and looking back at the gap he had narrowly escaped. "That was fucking close."

Swallowing a dry gulp, Jake nodded. "Are you okay, man?"

"I think so." He patted himself down. "I think—"

The ground shook again and the ledge behind them started to crumble. Tom pulled on Jake's arm and half-dragged him away from the edge. "We've got to go, Jake."

When Jake tried to stand, his legs gave way beneath him and he crumpled back down.

Using both hands, Tom grabbed him again. "Come on."

Jake let the big man pull him to his feet He draped his arm, and most of his body weight, over his friend's shoulder.

As they hobbled up the hill, the ground shook more and a mini landslide of bricks and debris rushed down towards them. When he looked at Tom, who was red-faced from the effort, Jake said, "I'm sorry, man. I'm a liability. You should have left me."

With his jaw locked tight and his feet slipping beneath him, Tom grimaced. "Shut up, Jake."

When they reached the top of the hill, Tom launched Jake with such force his feet left the ground. Jake screamed as he spun through the air. The breath left his lungs when he collided with a steel girder and nausea gripped his churning stomach.

Fighting to breathe, he watched Tom sway at the top of the hill and then fall forwards.

After a couple of minutes, Jake found his breath and lifted his head to look over at his immobile friend. "Thank you for saving me… again."

Tom didn't move.

"Tom, are you okay?"

Nothing.

"Tom?"

"Tom?"

"Tom?"

"T—"

Tom looked up, a heavy frown crushing his long face, and said, "I'm fine, stop fucking barking my name. You sound like a yappy dog."

Falling flat on his back again, Jake adjusted his glasses and stared up into the storm. The sound of destruction over the hill was moving away from them. Were they safe? Probably not in this fucking world.

It felt like only seconds had passed before his view of the sky was filled with Tom, but Jake knew it was a lot longer. The tall man peered down at him; the rage had left his face. "How are you feeling?"

Sitting upright so quickly his head spun, Jake rested his hands on the ground to steady himself. The scarf covering his face made it hard to breathe, but to remove it would fill his mouth with grit. Fighting against his pain, Jake started to cry. "I can't do it, Tom. I can't go any farther."

After tutting, Tom dropped down into a crouch and shoved Jake in the chest.

Jake's shoulder blades smashed against the jagged ground as he fell back. Before he could say anything, Tom grabbed and then lifted his right leg. Pulling air in through his teeth, Jake stared at the sky again and winced.

"What hurts on here?"

"Knee," was all he could manage before biting down hard on his bottom lip.

Tom extended and bent his leg several times, the movement sending stabbing pains through Jake's kneecap.

Grabbing his other leg, Tom asked, "And here?"

"Shin," Jake wheezed as heat rushed to his face, turning his skin clammy.

When Tom rubbed his shin, Jake wailed at the sky. "What the fuck are you doing, man?"

Tom stood up. "They're both fine."

Jake opened his mouth, but Tom cut him off, "I don't doubt they hurt, but nothing's broken. You can walk on them."

More tears stung his eyes, and Jake shook his head. "I can't."

When the ground rumbled behind them again, Tom glanced over his shoulder before looking back down at his friend. "You have to, Jake. If you don't, we're dead. Do you understand that?"

"Go without me, Tom."

Raising a clenched fist, Tom glared down at his friend. "I just risked my bloody life for you. If you say that again…"

A boom exploded behind them. It was so loud Jake imagined the earth's tectonic plates shifting. As the low thunder of it died down, the hissing of a thousand boiling lobsters screamed into the sky.

Instead of running, Tom looked at Jake and raised his eyebrows. "That was the last one."

"How can you be sure?"

Tom shrugged. "Dunno. But I'm sure." He looked calmer than he had in a long time. He then walked back up the hill, Jake presumed to look at the devastation.

As he watched his friend's back, Jake trusted Tom's assertion that his legs would hold and forced himself to his feet. Once he was upright, he wobbled for a moment before walking up the hill too; wincing with every step as if his bones were made of glass.

All he could see from the top of the hill was a hole where the ground used to be. It stretched so far and wide it was like staring off a cliff overlooking an abyss. It was so dark Jake couldn't see the writhing mass anymore. "Do you really think it's finished?"

Tom nodded.

"And," Jake said, turning to his friend, the wind rocking him on his feet, "do you still think nothing was following us?"

Tom lifted his lip in a snarl, shook his head, turned and walked back down the hill.

***

Although she'd watched Tom walk away from the edge, she still repeated, "Push him. Push him. Push him." Punching her thigh with the repetition, she barely felt the dull thud.

After she was done staring up at Jake while he looked off what was now a cliff, she dropped her head and spoke to her lap. "Half of the city falls and Tom fucking walks away from it. Why can't he just bloody die?"

Lifting her stinging eyes up to see Jake again, she asked herself the same question that had been in her thoughts constantly. Could she kill him when the time came?

Chapter Nine

When Tom stopped and stamped his foot on the rough ground, Jake's frame sagged in anticipation of what he knew was coming. They'd been walking for a day now, and Tom hadn't stopped complaining.

"I can't believe they stole my fucking water. I was trying to save your life, and the bastards stole my water!"

The burn in Jake's legs was easing, but it was hard to get going again once he'd stopped. He slowed down and hoped Tom would move off to save him the pain.

He didn't.

Grinding to a halt, Jake winced as his joints seized. "Are you sure you didn't bring it back over the hill with you when you came to rescue me? Everything happened quite quickly."

"Don't patronise me, Jake. I set it down before coming back for you. When we returned, it was gone. If you were made of stronger stuff, I'd still have it."

Looking at his friend's long face, Jake shook his head. "All right, Seabiscuit, ease off, will ya?" Leaning down, he rubbed his sore kneecap.

"Don't call me that."

The angrier Tom got, the longer his face hung. Not knowing whether to offer him a sugar cube or an apology, Jake gave neither.

Staring over at the blurred red tower on the horizon, Tom brushed his hair out of his eyes. "They're playing a bloody game with us. They give us hope and then steal it away just to fuck with us."

Jake swallowed the frothy saliva in his mouth. Tom wasn't the only one in need of a drink. "Maybe it rolled away when the ground shook?"

"Why are you sticking up for them?"

"Fucking hell, Tom, rein it in. I'm just suggesting there may be another explanation. Why does everything have to be a fucking conspiracy?"

With his face locked in a frown, Tom stared back in the direction from where they'd come.

Jake looked at his friend through narrowed eyes and cleared his throat. It brought bitter phlegm onto the back of his tongue so he lifted the scarf covering the lower half of his face and spat it out. "What did you see chasing me?"

"This again? Really? And you think I'm paranoid?"

"I know you're paranoid. That doesn't change the fact that you obviously saw something. All you ever do is look behind you now."

The wind tossed the loose bits of Tom's hair that refused to stay in his ponytail. Turning to face the tower, he threw an arm in its direction. "We've kept that bloody thing on our left-hand side for the past two years. Your plan isn't working!"

"What's that got to do with the things following us?"

"Your plan has everything to do with everything. It's our reason for being."

"Well, Mr. Ed, do you have a better plan?" When Tom didn't reply, Jake continued, "The idea was to—"

"I know what the idea was, but it hasn't worked, has it?"

Grinding his jaw, the popping of the grit in between his teeth amplifying through his skull, Jake showed his friend his palm. "Hang on a minute; we decided together that we'd do that. We need to stay in Birmingham, remember?"

Tom dropped his head in an impatient nod.

"And we only have one consistent landmark to get our bearings from."

Tom nodded again.

"The reason we need to stay in Birmingham is because we think Rory's still here, correct?"

"Think? What do you mean 'think'?"

"Sorry, Rory's in Birmingham."

For the first time in the past day, the tension fell from Tom's face. "Do you think he's been swallowed by one of the sinkholes?"

Suddenly, Jake saw the truth of Tom's anxiety. He shook his head. "No."

"How can you be so sure?"

"I can't, but I think Rory's out there, alive and well."

"And what if he's not?"

Jake stepped closer to Tom and looked into his foggy eyes. "I read a book once called *Man's Search for Meaning*. It was by a Jew who survived the holocaust in a prisoner of war camp."

"What's that got to do with my son?"

"The man was a psychiatrist. The book was his assessment of what he believed to be the reason that some people survived in the camps while others didn't."

Throwing a shrug, Tom said, "Which was…?"

"Meaning."

Tom stared at Jake.

"Those who had meaning in their life—a reason to exist—were the ones who survived."

"And Rory's my meaning?"

"Exactly. We haven't seen his corpse, so we have to keep going."

When Tom flinched, Jake raised an apologetic hand. "Sorry, but it's true. The only way we can assume he's still alive is because we have no evidence to the contrary."

Looking back over to the tower on the horizon, Tom ground his jaw. "I want to believe that—more than I've ever wanted to believe anything in my entire life." Sighing, Tom continued to stare into the distance.

Jake moved close to his friend and put his hand on his slumped back. "Believe it then. Reality is a choice. Choose your reality."

The silence lasted for a good few minutes before Jake finally said, "So we're looking for a Birmingham City football shirt, yeah?"

Tom's mouth was still frowning when he looked up at his friend but it quickly disappeared and he snorted a laugh. "Piss off."

Grinning, Jake threw his arms wide and the wind smashed into him. Finding his balance and grimacing from the pain in his legs, he shrugged. "I thought you were Birmingham through and through?"

A smile raised one side of Tom's mouth. "There's only one team in Birmingham, Jake, and it isn't City. And before you say it, it ain't West Brom either!" Looking away again, he sighed.

"I suppose none of that's important anymore though. Football used to be a religion for me," he squinted as he looked at the tower, "before all of this."

Refusing to let his friend forget his purpose, Jake said, "So we're looking for red hair?"

"You know what we're looking for. Stop being an idiot."

"And he has a cleft palette?"

Pushing the loose strands of hair from his eyes, Tom didn't reply.

"He's wearing one of your old Aston Villa shirts?"

"And he's going to be about seventeen now." Tom's voice wavered and his eyes welled up. "Seventeen! It's been a year since we've seen him and four since he put that bloody headset on!"

He stared at the tower again and he shook his head. "Four years is a long time. Why didn't they leave us alone when we were with them last? They're my family, not the property of Rixon International Limited. Arseholes. Sometimes I wish we'd stayed where we were."

"We would have died if we didn't run, Tom."

Tom regarded Jake with lifeless eyes. He was clearly aware of that fact.

Jake moved closer, clenched his jaw against the pain of his rusty joints screaming a burning protest, and dropped an arm over his friend's shoulder.

"Come on, man," Jake said. "Let's keep moving."

***

Staring at Jake as he hobbled off with Tom, she ran her tongue over her cracked lips. Why did he have to be so kind to his friend? What she had to do would be so much easier if Jake was a dick.

Chapter Ten

The woman's large body was spread over the rocky ground like fresh dough. She was naked save for a small shred of what looked like the remains of a woollen jumper clinging to her wrist. Varicose veins pooled in her arms and her skin was pale.

Jake looked up and scratched his beard as he scanned the surrounding storm for Bots. "Have you noticed how there are so many less gamers about now? I swear there were ten times as many only a few months ago."

Without replying, Tom also scanned their surroundings.

"Tom?"

There was a distant look to the man as he said, "Why are we helping them? They're in a better state than we are."

"At least we're conscious."

"Exactly! They're far better off. They say ignorance is bliss and New Reality makes that statement truer than ever. Ignorance is heaven now." He shook his head. "I can't keep spending what little energy I have making the lives of these idiots better."

The woman they stood over was in her late thirties to early forties. The only thing Jake could be certain of when it came to her physical health was that she was still breathing. Watching her chest rise and fall, he scratched his head. "What else can we do?"

Turning on his friend, Tom's eyes lit up. "Let's try and take her headset off."

When Jake's mouth fell open, he felt grateful for the scarf or he'd have been funnelling grit. Staring at his friend, he couldn't find the words to reply.

Tom shrugged. "So we know how to do it when we find Rory."

"But that might kill her."

"Rather her than my son."

The logic made sense. Jake knelt down next to the gamer and looked closely at the headset. Rolls of doughy fat belched from beneath it. The device looked like it had fused to the top half of her head. "How do you think we can get it off?"

"We could just rip it off."

"Rip it off?" The thought made Jake's already weak legs wobble. "That would kill her for certain." When Jake looked up at his tall friend, he was met with a cold stare. Although Tom hated talking about Thalia, Jake felt like he'd have to remind him what happened.

Tom shoved the woman's fat arm with his boot. "It'd put the bitch out of her misery."

"You do realise what you're saying, right?"

"Of course I realise." He pointed down at the woman. "Look at her, Jake; she's fucked anyway."

"What's wrong with you, Tom? Why would you want to kill an innocent person? Where's this coming from? This isn't you. Also," Jake pointed at the Rixon Tower on the horizon, "have you forgotten about our corporate overlords?"

Without replying, Tom looked to where Jake pointed. Biting down on a fingernail, he began to throw glances out in random directions. "We got away with it once before. Besides, would it really matter if she died? We'd probably be doing her a favour. Speed things up for her."

"What if you're wrong about Rixon? What if they're not interfering with everything we do in this world? Besides, what has this woman ever done to you?"

Tom didn't reply.

Jake lifted one of her heavy arms and arranged it so it covered an exposed breast. The touch of her cold and waxy skin made him shudder. It was like moving a corpse.

As Jake watched her large chest swell and subside with her breathing, the heavy, phlegmy death rattle sounding like it could stop at any moment, he wondered if Tom was right. Should they leave her be? She clearly didn't have long left.

"Well?" Tom barked, making Jake jump.

"Well what?"

"Shall we do it?"

"Do I really need to spell it out? No! Absolutely not! I'm not a murderer."

Jake could see the sneer even beneath Tom's scarf as he spoke. "But we are though, aren't we?"

"We didn't mean to kill Thalia. That wasn't murder. Not like you're suggesting now," Jake said.

Tom fell silent again and continued his search of their surroundings.

Jake planted his feet, buried his hands into her side, and gave her a hard shove. Grunting from the effort, he looked up at his disgruntled friend. "I need your help, Tom."

"Let's just leave her."

Jake stood up—his entire body popping, cracking and creaking in protest—and put his hands on his skinny hips. "What the hell's going on with you? What's all this bullshit about killing her? What's wrong with you today?"

It was only when Tom looked behind yet again that the light switched on in Jake's head. Clicking his fingers, he pointed at him. "You think it'll slow them down, don't you? You want to leave her as an offering."

Unable to hold eye contact, Tom looked away and mumbled, "No."

"You do. You want to leave her for them to feed on so we can get farther away."

"Well… it might work."

Dipping his head to get eye contact with Tom, Jake reached out and gave the top of Tom's skinny arm a squeeze. "Just tell me what you saw."

There was no reply.

"What if something happens to you? I need to know what I'm up against so I can defend myself."

A glaze washed over Tom's face—he wasn't letting Jake in.

Clapping his hands did little to snap his friend out of it so Jake continued, "Right, so we've decided that we're not going to kill her."

"You've decided that."

"Yes, I have. Now make yourself useful and help me."

"You do realise that you're probably not even helping, don't you?"

"You've already told me that turning them over is better than leaving them lying still. That's what they do in the hospitals, right?"

"Did, Jake, did."

"Whatever. Stop trying to get out of it and help me." Jake rolled his eyes, dropped into a hunch, and waited for Tom to squat down next to him.

When the tall man finally moved into place, Jake smiled. "See, there's a heart in there somewhere."

"It's not about kindness. I don't want help because of self-preservation. Why are we wasting energy on this fat slug? She decided to put the headset on."

"She's still a person."

"She's got all the sustenance she needs and we're living like rats."

"Then why are you helping?"

Tom looked at the floor. "If Rory's still out there, and if there are other people like us, I hope they're doing the same. I hope someone like you has passed him and taken an interest in his welfare."

Nodding, Jake said, "Karma."

"I believe in science, Jake. I'm not a nutter."

Jake laughed. They'd had the conversation too many times to repeat it.

Tom positioned himself so he was ready to push and groaned from the effort of crouching down.

"Right—three, two, one, go."

When Jake shoved her, the muscles in his back set alight and his head pulsed as if it was going to explode. With his feet scrabbling for positioning and his injured legs screaming for him to stop, he looked desperately at the gap between her back and the ground for any sign that they were making progress. "Come on, Tom. We can do this."

It was obvious that his friend didn't share his optimism.

"Imagine she's Rory."

The comment seemed to enrage the man, who growled as he pushed hard into her.

Seizing the opportunity, Jake put everything he had into it. Slowly, the large woman lifted from the ground a centimetre at a time.

The progress was steady until she neared her tipping point. With his hands sinking into her fat arm, sweat running down his forehead, and his vision swimming, Jake fought his shaking muscles and dug deep. If he dropped her now, she was never coming back up again.

When the sharp tang of excrement hit him, Jake looked down at the viscous paste rolling down her back and tried to breathe through his mouth.

Gritting his teeth and shoving harder than before, they got the woman past her balance point and she fell away from them. Knowing what was coming next; Jake mirrored Tom in stepping away from her and pushed the sunglasses up his sweaty nose.

When Tom shrieked, Jake looked at her exposed back. Hot saliva gushed down his throat as he stumbled backwards. Unable to look away, he stood limp-jawed and stared at it.

***

Her stomach bucked. What the hell? Turning away did nothing to banish the image that was now burned in her mind's eye. How did she get in that state? It wasn't often that she felt inclined to agree with Tom, but killing her probably would be for the best.

Chapter Eleven

The pressure sore was so big it stretched all the way across her sizeable lower back. Dark red and glistening with pus and filth, it wept out across her skin. It ran so deep that Jake peered in to see if he could see bone. After a few seconds, he had to turn away.

Several deep breaths did nothing to calm the nausea rolling through his guts; instead, it filled his sinuses with the smell of rotting flesh. Not even the fierce wind could dilute the rancid kick. Jake put all of his attention on trying to settle his stomach by turning away from the woman.

Tom walked around in front of Jake. "There's nothing we can do for this one. The sore is too bad."

"Is there really nothing?"

With a thick frown, Tom threw his hands up. "What do you want from me? It needs to be cleaned. She needs bedside care. We can't do that."

Looking back at the glistening wound, the grime of the world sticking to it and quickly turning it matt, Jake shook his head. "She's in such a bad way though."

"Exactly! What hope do we have of helping her? We don't even have clean water." Raising his voice, Tom looked at the tower. "*They* could do something about it. All they'd need to do is get one of their Bots to keep it clean."

Searching his friend's face, Jake put a hand on his slim shoulder. "Is this about them?"

"Them?"

"The things following us. The things you want to leave a dead body for."

Straightening his back, Tom gave a sharp shake of his head. "No. It's the truth. To treat this sore, you need a sterile environment. Look at it, Jake."

When Jake looked back, the angry red wound throbbed. Was it a trick of his exhausted imagination, or was it really happening?

"It also needs time and constant attention to give it a chance to heal."

When Jake frowned, Tom said, "I was a paramedic you know. I know what I'm talking about."

Jake gave a heavy sigh. "How long does she have left?"

"Dunno. The only thing I can say for sure is that there's nothing we can do to help her." Before he'd finished the sentence, Tom was looking back in the direction they'd come from. Clapping his hands together, he said, "Right, let's go."

It wasn't that he didn't trust his friend in this instance, he seemed genuine, but something kept Jake's feet rooted in place. Then he saw it.

Closing the distance between him and the woman, Jake crouched down next to her.

"Jake, I told you, there's nothing we can do. Come on, let's go," Tom said anxiously.

Leaning down so the gash was less than a metre from his face, Jake held his breath. The ground glistened where the sore had wept into the rubble. Wincing as he stretched his arm out, he lifted a particularly slimy and grime-covered brick.

"What the hell are you doing?"

Revulsion washed through him and his grip weakened, but not to the point where he dropped the brick. Flinging it to one side, he picked up the next lump of rubble. It was slipperier than the last, but he moved it aside to reveal the prize. Looking over at Tom, he pointed into the hole. "Coke, Tom, a full can of Coke."

The can was so slimy with secretions it was like lifting a wet bar of soap. Thinking he had a good grip on it, Jake stood up and it slipped from his grasp.

As he watched it spin through the air, seemingly moving in slow motion, Jake flinched. The can hit the ground, but there was no expected fizz of escaping liquid. Jake picked it back up, wiped it on his trousers, and walked over to Tom. "Want some?"

Staring at the can, Tom screwed his long nose up like he was close to violence. "What's wrong with you? It's been sat in her pus for God knows how long. There's no way I'm drinking that."

Shrugging, Jake tapped the top of the can. "More for me then."

He popped it open and was surprised to hear the hiss of carbonation. After lifting up his scarf he raised the glistening can to his mouth. All the while, he could feel Tom's penetrative stare. Just as it was about to touch his lips, his throat lifted from the inside and rejected the liquid before he'd even tasted it. "Damn it!" Throwing the can away, he watched the black liquid seep out. "Damn it!"

When Jake looked at Tom, he was met with a tight-lipped smile. "Not that thirsty then, eh?"

"Fuck off, Tom." Swallowing against the dry and gritty lump in his throat, he said, "Anyway, we drank yesterday, I'm sure we'll find something else soon."

The look on Tom's smug face made him want to swing for him, so he looked away and stared into the small hole he'd dug next to the woman.

What he saw made him instantly forget his frustration. "Oh, my God, Tom. Oh, my God."

Before Tom could reply, Jake was next to the woman again, throwing lumps of rubble to the side and digging a bigger hole.

###

It took about an hour, but by the time Jake had finished he'd cleared a patch that was about three metres square and sweat was gushing off him. His sore muscles ached again, his shoulders burned from the exertion, and the grit on the wind was sticking to his sweating face. But it was worth every drop of pain and discomfort. Staring back at him from the hole he'd created was a bent and buckled vending machine. It had taken a battering that had clearly spoiled a lot of its contents but there was still plenty left for them. Pulling his hair from his forehead, Jake nodded towards the hole. "See, Tom, this is our reward for looking after all of those poor gamers. Stick that in your scientific pipe and smoke it."

Tom shook his head. "Coincidence, Jake."

Unable to suppress his grin, Jake said, "Karma."

"Whatever. Any water?"

The bottom row where the water should have been was completely empty. Jake sighed. "No."

Grinding his jaw, Tom looked at the tower. "And you still think Rixon have nothing to do with this? When was the last time you came across a vending machine that had all of the water removed from it? They're fucking with us again!"

Wishing he had an argument didn't make it a reality.

Swiping his hand through the air as if he were batting away a fly, Tom said, "Anyway, just pass me anything without caffeine in it. I'm fed up with drinking Coke. It only makes me thirstier."

Retrieving two cans of Tango, Jake walked over to Tom and handed him one.

Guzzling the sweet, orange-flavoured syrup so hard it burned his throat, Jake then belched half of it back up into his mouth. There was a slight kick of bile as he swallowed it back down again, but the taste was mostly unaffected.

Jake quickly finished the can, tossed it, and the wind sent it skittering over the rubble. After watching it roll away, Jake burped, careful to keep the liquid in his stomach this time. "I feel like I could drink a swimming pool dry."

"Take it slow, Jake."

"All right, Mum."

Tom raised his hands. "I'm just saying. You'll make yourself sick if you carry on drinking it that quickly."

As if on cue, Jake's stomach rumbled, and he had to take several breaths to keep the liquid down. Turning his back on Tom so he could hide his discomfort, he then returned to the vending machine.

When he came back, he had five chocolate bars fanned out in his right hand. "Pick a bar, any bar."

The faintest smile cracked Tom's face.

It was good to see his friend happy. Jake glanced up at the gloomy sky, which was getting darker by the minute, then scratched his head and looked around. "It'll be night soon. We may as well lie down here until morning."

While opening a chocolate bar, Tom glanced around. "I'll only do it if we take shifts on guard. One of us should always be awake from now on."

"Okay, I understand. Now tell me what's been following us."

The bags on Tom's long face pulled it to the ground as he stared at his friend. He said nothing.

Shaking his head, Jake stretched his arms up in an attempt to force the lethargy from his aching body. "You look like you need it more, Tom. You sleep first."

***

They were stopping for the evening. Should she seize the opportunity? She could end it all now. It had to happen sooner or later. If not tonight, how long could she drag it out?

She watched them eat their chocolate and drink more fizzy drinks. She watched Tom lie down and fall asleep almost instantly. Rubbing her sore eyes, she watched Jake pace up and down.

She watched him stand still.

He sat down.

Once he was horizontal, his eyes slowly shut.

Her voice came out as a soft hiss. "Sweet dreams, Jake. Sweet dreams."

Chapter Twelve

Jake's eyes flashed open. Shit! How long had he been asleep? He lifted his head from its awkward position. A crick in his neck stabbed into the bottom of his skull and made him draw in a sharp breath as he looked over at his friend. Tom was still snoozing. Good.

It was as dark, dusty, and desolate as it had been when he'd passed out. Nothing had happened, thank God. He relaxed his shoulders and smiled to himself—. Jake pushed himself upright and rolled his burning shoulders in large circles. It did little to ease his discomfort.

The concrete slab he'd slept on had made his back so cold his spine felt like it had turned to ice. Hugging himself tightly, Jake sat there and shivered.

Jake squinted to try and make out his surroundings despite the wind smashing into his face and the pattering of grit hitting the lenses on his glasses. On the best of days, it was hard to see more than about fifty metres ahead. At night-time, exhausted and with a sugar-fuelled headache cramping his face, Jake was virtually blind. But he'd promised Tom that he'd act as look out. All he could do was make sure he didn't fall asleep again.

Swallowing a couple of times, Jake grimaced at the taste. The high-sugar diet and lack of dental hygiene left a layer of fur on his tongue. It tasted like bile, and no amount of running it across his teeth could banish it.

As Jake became more lucid, he started to feel his pounding heart. It was on the edge of a panic attack and worms of anxiety writhed in his guts. Why did he feel like this?

Then he heard it.

Gasping, he spun around.

It was close, but where?

A raspy, rattling wheeze breathed in his ear. Turning sharply, Jake still couldn't see a thing. Where was it?

He looked over at Tom. He was still asleep.

Then he heard a deep exhale and a satisfied, gravelly groan.

Where was it?

What was it?

With his skin turning to gooseflesh, Jake remained rooted to the spot and shook.

When the rubble shifted a few metres away, he snapped his legs back and pulled them beneath him as if he were about to lose them. The disturbance, a Mohawk of raised rubble, made a beeline for him like a shark's fin through water. Seconds before collision, it vanished.

Scanning around, Jake's heart galloped. What if another sinkhole opened up? What would he do? Should he wake Tom?

A puff behind him made him spin around to see an explosion of dust shoot from the ground.

Was it another one? One was bad enough.

Focusing on his breathing, his heart ready to explode, Jake remained sat on the flat lump of concrete.

The movement around him stopped, but Jake could still hear it. It was scrabbling beneath where he sat.

Looking down, Jake's stomach sank. He was sat on a headstone. No wonder it was the flattest surface in the vicinity. Running a shaking hand over its cold surface, he felt the engraved legend to someone passed. It was too dark to read it.

Keeping his palm on the inscription, he then felt a vibration on the other side, a prolonged scratching like someone dragging a trowel along it. Jake snapped his hand away.

Along with the slow dry rasp running through the slab, Jake heard the slapping of salivating jaws. His pulse rocketed.

Frozen to the spot and panic swelling in his chest, Jake held his breath for the length of every scratch. They seemed to last forever as they dragged along the underside of the concrete.

When Tom let out a loud snort in his sleep, Jake yelped.

The sound beneath him stopped.

Maybe it had gone. Maybe it was as scared of him as he was of it. Maybe—

Scraaaaaaaaaaatch!

It was impossible to guess how much time had passed, but if Jake were to give it a go, he'd say it had been about twenty minutes since the last scratch. Maybe he was alone again. Maybe he could finally move.

Looking across, he saw Tom was still sleeping. At least he'd missed the ordeal. It made no sense for him to have any more fear in his heart—Jake had enough for the both of them.

Jake's bladder ached. He had to get up. Looking around, he chewed his bottom lip. It was like being a child all over again. He used to wake in the middle of the night, desperate for a wee, but refused to get up because of the monster waiting for him beneath the bed. The second his small bare foot touched the carpet, it would grab his ankle and rip him under. It would drag him into the rubble and feast on him with wild savagery.

But Jake wasn't going to piss the bed this time. Just the thought of Tom waking and giving him the same worried look that he'd received from his parents every morning made him nervous. To utter the same words—'Isn't he a bit too old to piss the bed now?' Or 'we'll have to get him a rubber mattress.' They'd speak as if he wasn't there—as if he had no feelings.

MICHAEL ROBERTSON

He got to his feet, fatigue shaking his weak legs, and turned his back to the wind. Clumsily freeing himself from his trousers, he urinated with the flow of the gale. The hot liquid burned as it left his bladder, dehydration turning his piss thick. It felt like passing honey.

Putting himself away a little too soon, he felt a warm trickle run down the inside of his thigh. Jake sat back down on the slab, curled over, and rocked in the cold wind.

After sitting cross-legged for some time, Jake closed his eyes and focused on his breathing.

In. Pause. Out.

In. Pause. Out.

The distant barking of a fox rode on the wind. The sting of grit pattered against the side of his face. The smell of decomposition filled the air. The smell was always there, but he was so accustomed to the reek, he now had to focus to notice it.

In. Pause. Out.

In. Pause. Out.

With everything settling down, his heart stabilising and his muscles relaxing, Jake let his shoulders unwind.

When he opened his eyes again, he saw the dark night through the soft lens of meditative calm. The last of his tension had vanished. Everything was going to be okay. Maybe it was just a bad dream. That must have been it, just a—

Scraaaatch.

96

***

Continuing to shape her fingernails, she ran them across the rough surface. *Scraaatch. Scraaatch. Scraaaaaaaatch.*

Jake wouldn't sleep tonight but that was all that would happen... for now.

Hopefully, his fear would drive him from the city and she wouldn't have to deal with him at all.

Chapter Thirteen

When Jake opened his eyes, the diluted daylight burned them and sent sharp pains tearing through his sinuses. Snapping them shut again, he let out a long groan. The last thing he remembered was sitting upright and shaking from the cold as he strained to hear over the howling wind. After being sat like that for a few hours with no sign of the creature, he must have drifted off again.

Lying on the cold slab, Jake reopened his eyes slowly and stared up. The grey clouds above churned like the cogs of a giant machine. Drawing a deep breath, he released another exasperated sigh. How much more of this could he take?

Finally finding the motivation to move, Jake sat up. He crossed his legs, scratched his head, and continued squinting. The sunglasses seemed ineffectual, but he wasn't prepared to take them off to test that theory.

Running his tongue around the inside of his mouth sent an electric buzz straight into his jawbone. He winced and clamped his hand across his face. Three or four teeth in the back left corner of his mouth had turned so sensitive that he couldn't eat on that side now. It was at its worst when he first woke in the morning, and it was getting worse every day. How long would it be before the other side felt the same? Swallowing back the stale taste of halitosis, the bitter tang of decay now a permanent resident on his tongue, he wondered if he'd be sucking his food by the end of the month.

When he looked around and saw the disturbed rubble from the previous night, his stomach tensed. Last night had happened; it wasn't a hideous nightmare, regardless of how much he wished it was. Glancing across at his friend, he saw Tom was still sleeping. The long hike had taken a lot out of both of them.

Jake stood up and his muscles ached in protest. When he looked down and saw the headstone, he froze. He shook his head, rubbed his eyes, and reread the inscription.

Jake Weston

Good friend. Dearly missed.

19th November 2048 -

The other date was illegible. Deep scratches that looked like claw marks tore through it. Jake shook where he stood and continued to look at the headstone. Why was it crossed out? What date was on there?

Jake wobbled as he was battered by the ragged wind. He tilted his head to the side, narrowed his eyes, and rubbed the date with his foot—none of which helped him read it any better.

He looked at the line of raised rubble again; his eyes following it away from where he stood while he searched for movement. Seeing nothing other than storms, he dropped into a painful crouch, picked up a handful of the finer bits of ruin around him, and covered his name over. Tom didn't need to see it. He already had enough on his mind.

He stood back up and glanced at the vending machine. The supplies could wait until both he and Tom were ready to load up.

Jake walked over to his sleeping friend and prodded him with the toe of his boot.

When Tom's bloodshot eyes opened, Jake scratched his head and remarked, "You look like shit, man. Are you okay?"

Lying still, his normally tightly tied hair dancing in the breeze, Tom groaned and rubbed his face. "My head hurts. I'm not sure I can go anywhere yet."

"We have to keep moving."

"Just give me five minutes," Tom sighed.

Glancing around, Jake shook his head. "No."

The fog lifted from Tom's features, and he craned his neck to follow Jake's gaze. "What did you see?"

"Nothing." The reply was quick; too quick.

Every trace of tiredness had left Tom at this point. "What did you see?"

"Nothing. We need to find Rory, don't we?"

Tom nodded and sat up, grimacing with the movement.

Handing him a can of Sprite, Jake shrugged at the distaste on Tom's long face. "There are other choices in the machine."

Tom took the drink, looked at the tower, and said ruefully, "They purposefully took the water from that vending machine. I know it. They did it to fuck with us. That's all they seem interested in doing. Arseholes."

The end of Tom's sentence barely registered when Jake looked down and saw he was lying on a slab similar to the one he'd been on. Looking Tom square in the eyes, he clapped his hands. "Right, come on, man. Let's go."

Tom held up his free hand, drained the can of Sprite, and said, "Chill out, yeah? I'm moving."

As he watched Tom get to his feet, Jake winced in sympathy. If Tom felt anywhere near as bad as he did, then he was going through hell right now. "So what did you dream about?"

Looking up, Tom scowled. "What?"

"What did you dream about last night?"

"My wife and son." The anger left his voice. "I dream about them every night."

Jake nodded and said, "This is going to be the day, Tom. I can feel it. We're going to find Rory."

"Don't play with my emotions."

"We've got to be positive. Law of attraction and all that."

"Law of what?"

"Like attracting like. You manifest what you focus on."

Tom shook his head and scoffed. As he walked off, he called over his shoulder, "Whatever."

Holding back, Jake looked down.

Tom DiFool

A father. A husband. The best friend a man could hope for.

10th April 2045—10th April 2077

The letters blurred and Jake swallowed the lump in his throat.

***

As she watched Jake stare at the headstone, she smiled and rubbed her hands together. It wouldn't be long. "What a wonderful birthday surprise!"

Chapter Fourteen

Snapping from his daze, Jake lifted his head to see his friend walking away. He looked down at the headstone one last time and he cleared his throat. "Tom, wait up!"

Tom stopped and turned around.

Jake pointed towards the vending machine. "We need to take supplies."

Although Tom hesitated a few seconds, he gave Jake a sombre nod.

"I'm not excited about living off that shit either, but what other choice do we have?"

Jake was answered again with the same sombre nod—at least it was an affirmative response.

Walking over to the exposed machine, Tom a few paces behind, Jake heard his friend slip. When he turned around, he saw him standing on one leg. "Are you okay?"

Tom gritted his teeth and frowned hard. "I think I've fucked my ankle up. I hate this fucking place. I hate Rixon. I hate that I can't be around my family."

"Come on, keep your chin up. Let's keep moving. We'll find Rory."

"Don't tell me to keep my chin up. I've been keeping my chin up for four fucking years now." His face had turned red. "How much longer do I have to hold it up for?"

"Let's just get our supplies and keep moving, yeah?"

As Jake picked his way over the terrain, he glanced at the gamer they'd turned over. The deep sore on her back was plugged with grit. Shuddering, Jake peered into the hole at the vending machine. A chill ran through his veins and the woman was completely forgotten. "Shit!"

When Tom appeared next to him, Jake winced in anticipation of his friend's reaction.

"What the fuck? Where's all the fucking food and drink gone?"

Jake was speechless and continued to stare at the carcass of the vending machine.

Red faced and shaking, Tom threw his middle finger at the tower. His voice cracking as he shouted, "Fuck you, Rixon!"

Tom picked up a rock and lobbed it in the direction of their corporate overlord. "Fuck you, you fucking arseholes! Fuck you!"

Jake gaped at the hole in the back of the machine—the metal was folded in as if a powerful punch had blown through it. With how the machine lay, that powerful punch would have had to have been from beneath it; from something *underground.*

Circumnavigating the hole, Tom strode towards the tower. "Fucking Rixon. Fucking arseholes!"

As long as he wasn't looking into the hole, Jake didn't care. Let him think Rixon did this to them. An icy chill ran through Jake as he studied the scratch marks that cut through the red metal to the steel beneath. It was as if something with clawed hands had reached up and scrabbled away as it pulled itself through. The memory of last night sent a shiver through him. *Scratch. Scratch. Scratch.*

It was clear to see the hole was the entrance to a tunnel. Jake's eyes found the raised spine of disturbed rubble a few metres away where he imagined the path of it would have followed. Scratching his head, he glanced at Tom, who was still preoccupied with venting his anger at the tower. How could he tell him? The poor man would never sleep again if he knew what had happened in the night.

When Tom returned, Jake stepped away from the hole.

Jake saw what Tom was about to do. Seconds before he could land his kick aimed at the gamer's headset, Jake jumped on him and pulled him back in time to watch his foot catch nothing but air.

The struggle was hard but he managed to restrain his friend and pull him back a few paces.

"What are you doing, Tom? Do you want to get shot at?"

"They're fucking arseholes! They're fucking with us, so we give up." With wide eyes, Tom looked over at the tower again. "Well, you know what? I ain't ever giving up. I'm going to find my son and then I'm coming for them."

Ushering Tom away while watching the ground to make sure neither of them fell, Jake managed to turn him around. "Come on, we need to get out of here. We need to find Rory."

As they walked off, Jake glanced back. They were now far enough away from Tom's grave but looking at the fat gamer made Jake's palms start sweating as he thought about what Tom had nearly done. The last thing they needed was the Bots on top of them too.

From their current position, Jake was able to get a better look at the raised line of rubble. The path led up to the vending machine, seemed to loop around and head back to the area of the sinkhole. Maybe the thing last night was just a scout. Maybe it had taken the food back to its pack and Jake happened to be in the way of the expedition. It could have simply been a coincidence. Wrong place, wrong time? Or maybe the vending machine was a bonus, and he and Tom were the true prizes. Maybe it had gone to tell the rest of the herd that it had found them.

Jake snapped out of his daydream with a jolt when Tom stopped and said, "What are you looking at?"

"Hm? Uh, nothing." He shook his head and drew a shaky breath. "Nothing."

Tom stared at his friend through narrowed eyes, looked back to where Jake had been looking, and then a frown crushed his long face.

Imagining the things watching them and lurking beneath as they positioned themselves to strike; Jake tugged on Tom's sleeve. "Come on. Let's keep moving."

***

Why didn't they just bloody give up?

Why did she have to be the one to end it all?

She rubbed her tired eyes as she watched them walk away and let out a deep sigh at the inevitability of their situation. She had to be the one to take responsibility—someone had to.

Popping the ring pull, the carbonated hiss revealing the freshness of the drink despite its dented exterior, she lifted it to her lips and tasted the sweet liquid.

Someone had to end it all.

Chapter Fifteen

Every step sent shooting pains up Jake's shins. When would his legs give way completely? Exhaustion had turned his jaw slack and sent his shoulders south as he plodded on.

Swallowing hard, his dry throat itched and the stirrings of a hacking cough crawled at the back of it. Jake looked up at the sky and saw it had turned from gunmetal grey to black. Butterflies of anxiety shimmered in his stomach; at some point, the cloak of night would envelop them again and they'd have to stop and rest.

When he looked ahead at the haggard Tom walking along the ridge of a deep crater with the rags he called clothes billowing out behind him, Jake could only assume he looked just as bad. If anyone saw them from a distance, they'd think they were ghosts—much more of this existence and that's exactly what Tom and Jake would become.

Not only was every step setting fire to his lower legs, but every step demanded Jake's attention as the ground slipped and shifted. The concentration required to stay upright and the loud roar of the wind made it hard to keep looking for Rory.

The silence between the pair had lasted for hours so when Tom spoke, Jake latched onto it. "Why are there so many less gamers about?"

The memory of last night flooded Jake's mind. *Scratch.* He shuddered and then shook his head as if to dislodge the image of claws dragging fat bodies into the rubble. "I don't know, man. Maybe the lack of exercise and fattening diet is killing them off."

"Why now?"

Jake shrugged. "Maybe we've past the average life expectancy for gamers."

The crater next to them was so huge it could have concealed a shopping mall. Looking into it, Tom sighed. "Do you think Rory's gone?"

"No."

"No?"

"If I think Rory's gone, then why are we looking for him? If there's a chance, we have to keep moving. He's your son, Tom. We have to keep going."

"I will, but what's keeping you going, Jake?"

"I've already told you."

"Nature? Are you still trying to convince me that you're doing all of this to find a fucking tree?"

"I've told you, Tom, I didn't travel when I had the chance before all of this. We lived on such a beautiful planet, and it's taken the destruction of it to make me realise what I was taking for granted. I want to survive long enough to see change. I want to see the start of this world returning to its former beautiful glory. Besides," Jake pointed down, "this is reality."

Tom's sneer was visible regardless of the scarf covering half of his face. "I don't think it'll be that long before things start to change. Once all the gamers die, those arseholes will scuttle out of the towers and remake the world in their own image. It'll be paradise with so few people left, but it'll be built on the bones of humanity."

Jake shrugged. "Maybe… or maybe there's no one in there other than a few operators. Either way, at some point, nature will fight back. I know it." Smiling at his friend, he dipped a nod at him. "Until then, it would be an honour to see my best friend reunited with his son."

"Best friend?"

"Come on, Tom. We've spent so long together now." The words stuck in his throat, but it wasn't because he didn't mean them. This could be their last few days together and Tom needed to know how he felt. "I love you like a brother. You've kept me going, man."

"If you love me like a brother, then why don't you tell me about your past? About your family?"

Just thinking about his family weighed Jake down. "There's nothing to say about them, Tom. I'm closer to you than I ever was to them."

Tom looked away, his flimsy frame rocking in the wind. There was so little meat on his bones he looked like he'd snap if he fell hard enough.

Clearing his throat, Jake's voice cracked. "You've been a rock for me, Tom. I wouldn't have found the strength to continue over the past few years if it wasn't for you and your family. Your meaning has become my meaning. I want to help you find Rory and get him out of New Reality."

Seeing his friend's eyes glaze, Jake continued, "You're a good man. You're kind, strong, and compassionate. You're the best friend anyone could ask for."

After absentmindedly kicking a stone, Jake continued, "I know you won't talk about the things following us because of how scary they are. I get that. I know you want to protect me. I've heard you screaming at night and I know you're trying to keep me from having the same nightmares."

Regarding his friend with his grey eyes, Tom then glanced behind them, scanning the wasteland like he had done since their first encounter with the creatures. "You're right, you don't need to know."

"I love you, Tom."

Tom looked away and cleared his throat. "Right, you soppy bastard, let's keep going."

As the next few hours passed, the pair trudged on. Jake's confession of his platonic love for Tom had created an atmosphere. Although Tom was a loyal and incredibly caring friend, discussing his emotions was a step too far for him. Walking a few paces ahead, he glanced behind frequently but avoided eye contact with Jake.

When Jake heard shifting rubble behind him, he spun around. With his mouth turning from dry to arid, he searched the thick dust clouds, his upper body tense. It was impossible to see anything. Jake stood still and strained his ears over the howling wind.

Nothing.

No more shifting ground.

No line of raised rubble.

Any sniff of them being followed, and he was confessing everything to Tom about the night before.

It seemed that Tom was oblivious to the sound Jake had heard, the gap between the two having increased during Jake's momentary pause. Quickening his pace, Jake caught up with his friend. Desperate to break the tension between them and still unsure as to what he'd say to him, he tapped Tom on the back.

Tom spun around with a deep frown on his face.

Trying to catch his breath, Jake said, "Um... do you think Rixon control the air we breathe?"

Just the mention of their nemesis was enough to wind Tom tight. "I think they control everything. I think they could turn us off like a light in an instant."

"Then why haven't they? Surely if they control the air, all they'd need to do is shut it off and we wouldn't be a problem to them anymore."

The frown remained on Tom's face. "Maybe we're not a problem. Maybe we're entertainment. Besides, if they shut the air off, it would also kill the gamers."

"And they give a fuck about them?"

"How many times do you want to have this conversation, Jake? I don't think they want to murder them."

Jake shook his head. "I don't think they control everything." Looking around, he opened his arms wide. "What if we just happen to be in the armpit of the world?"

"Birmingham's always been the armpit of the world. What's your point?"

Checking behind again, Jake said, "I bet there are trees and forests somewhere. I like to think the rain forests are still intact. The waterfalls are still falling. The glaciers still splitting and shifting."

Tom scoffed.

"But what if I'm right? What if they *don't* have a grip on everything? What if it's just Birmingham?"

Throwing his hands up, Tom shrugged. "Well, if you are right, I hope you find them after we've found Rory."

Jake raised his eyebrows. "Me? Don't you mean us? All of us will find them."

"If Rory's as fucked as all of the other gamers—which I'm sure he is—then I'll need to stay with him until he's better."

A pain tore through Jake's heart as he felt his dream slipping from his grasp. What an idiot. Of course Rory would need rehabilitation. Why didn't he think about that sooner?

The panic passed. If the headstone was anything to go by, then Tom wasn't long for this earth so there was no point in getting het up about a future that probably wouldn't exist. Time and dates meant very little now but if he were to guess, Jake was pretty sure Tom's birthday wasn't far away. They'd be lucky to have found Rory by then.

"You're right, Tom. It will be quite a rehabilitation." It felt like an empty promise, but he made it anyway. "I'll stay with you guys and do everything I can to help."

A watery glaze covered Tom's eyes as he searched Jake's face. "Are you sure?"

The image of the headstone filled Jake's mind's eye again. Swallowing the lump in his throat, he nodded.

Tom reached out and rested his hand on Jake's shoulder. He glanced around for a moment and then looked back at Jake. His eyes held a hint of the brilliant blue that once shone from them as he quietly said, "Thank you."

***

It would be appropriate to feel sorry for Tom, but she didn't. As she watched him, she suddenly became aware of her twisting face. The sight in front of her left a bad taste in her mouth. Clinging onto Jake, Tom clearly hoped he'd stay with him on his pointless mission.

Whether Tom found his son or not was not her concern; it was Jake that mattered. Regardless of how much Tom distracted Jake, she wasn't going to fall into that same trap. To see Tom as anything other than an obstruction was foolish. After all, if she had to end Jake's life it would be because of Tom holding him back. Compassion wasn't an emotion she could afford to give to the tall man—it wasn't one that Jake could afford to give either.

Chapter Sixteen

"Not far to go, Tom. I can actually see the top of this bloody hill at last," Jake said after looking up to where they were heading.

His head was spinning and stars were swimming before his eyes when he looked back to check on Tom. He saw that he had his friend's attention but the red-faced man didn't reply.

The area was littered with bones; it wasn't the first time they'd come across a place like this.

"More bones, Tom." Laughing, and then fighting to catch his breath, Jake said, "I didn't realise climbing this hill was so hard."

Tom still didn't reply.

With his eyes already stinging from the sweat and grit that had run into them, Jake pushed on. He stumbled on a raised lump of rubble and sharp pains ran up his legs as he fought for balance.

"Walking over this shit is doing my bloody head in," he grumbled.

Turning around again, he saw Tom had stopped. It was the perfect excuse to do the same. Resting his hands on his knees, he hunched over and drew air into his lungs.

When Jake looked up, he saw Tom glance down the hill and then back to the patch of bones on the floor by his feet. With wide eyes, he repeated the action, lingering slightly longer on the bones.

"What have you seen, Tom?"

Without replying, Tom walked up the hill towards him.

"Tom? What's going on, man? What have you seen?"

Still no reply.

When Tom was next to him, Jake grabbed his skinny arm. Pulling his friend towards him, he said, "Tell me what's going on in your head."

There was a shake running through Tom as he looked down the hill again. "I hadn't thought about it until now."

"Thought about what? What are you talking about?"

With his face as white as the bleached calcium surrounding them, Tom shivered. "The patches of bones. Why we keep coming across areas littered with them. I'd used it as a chance to educate you on which bone was which, but I didn't see the obvious." Losing focus, he rubbed his chin. "I didn't see the bigger picture."

The ground shifted beneath Jake again, and he had to throw his arms out to maintain his balance. "Come on, man, spit it out before I fall back down this bloody hill."

Smacking his own head with the heel of his palm, Tom seemed lost in his thoughts. "Why didn't I see it? I'm such an idiot."

Before he could restrain himself, Jake shook him. "What's going on?"

"The patches of bones, Jake."

"You've already said that."

"So many bones in one place, then none for miles, then another patch."

"And?"

"Jesus, Jake, isn't it obvious? These are feeding grounds!"

Jake's blood turned cold. He'd been ignoring that same nagging thought but with Tom saying it so directly, it was unavoidable. From his elevated vantage point, the path they'd taken up the hill looked very different. Each pile of bones had ridges leading away from them like the spokes of a wheel. Ridges made by burrowing creatures. Ridges like the one he was currently stood on.

Jake jumped away from it and continued looking down the hill. On closer inspection, he saw scratches—much like the ones he saw on the vending machine—on some of the lumps of concrete closest to the bones.

Images flicked through his mind. Flesh being torn free. Gnashing jaws. Dripping blood. "Tell me what you saw chasing me, Tom. Tell me what we're up against." *Tell me what kept me awake last night.*

Tom shook his head. "We need to keep moving."

Jake looked down the hill again, visibility was still no better than about fifty metres. He felt the strength drain from his legs as he wondered if he could keep going.

"Do you think they're following us?" he asked fearfully.

Bouncing on the balls of his feet, Tom grimaced as if waiting around was causing him physical pain. "Come on, Jake. We need to go."

Jake flicked his head up, and held his breath for a second. "Did you just hear that? It sounded like shifting rubble."

What little colour Tom had in his skin vanished. Shaking his head, he set off up the hill again.

"Are they following us, Tom? They could have been on our heels for days and we wouldn't see them through this bloody storm."

"Why do you think I want to keep moving?" Tom called over his shoulder.

Looking at the bones again, Jake's sinuses were suddenly alive with the metallic tang of blood. He could almost taste it himself as if he were part of their ritual. It was as though the essence of the feast hung in the air.

Jake covered his mouth and nose, looked down the hill one last time, and then bent over to pick up a steel pole. He looked at the jagged end from where it had broken free, thought for a moment, and then dropped it again, the loud clang making Tom spin around. If they wanted to attack them, they would; carrying a stupid pole would just slow him down.

Spinning around, Jake followed his friend.

***

She frowned as she watched on. It had taken Jake a long time to recognise the piles for what they were. Did he even see the scratch marks on the bones? They'd been damaged by sharp nails resting on them as they were picked clean of every inch of flesh.

Maybe that's how Tom should go; eaten alive, his throat torn out first so he couldn't scream. Clenching her jaw, she imagined the pressure of her bite breaking his windpipe. It would be his birthday soon. That could be his gift.

Chapter Seventeen

A strange sense crept into Jake's dreams, a nagging feeling that he was being watched—that *they* were watching him. Opening his eyes, he gasped when he saw Tom staring down at him; his long face just inches away. He scrabbled backwards and the rough ground bit into his back as he breathed heavily. "What is it, Tom? What's wrong?"

The bags beneath Tom's eyes were packed and his skin was pale. "We need to go." He looked behind him. "We need to go now."

Swallowing back the funky taste in his mouth, his sticky saliva doing nothing to dilute it, Jake sat up. Squinting against the ache in his sinuses, he rubbed below his eyes to try and ease the congestion. "Right, calm down and tell me what's happened."

Tom stood to his full height, scratched his head with a shaking hand, and looked around. His eyes not settling on any one spot, he said, "Just trust me, we need to go now."

By the time Jake got to his feet, his shins on fire and hips burning, he found himself already staring at his friend's back. "Wait up, man. Just tell me what's going on."

When Tom didn't respond and continued to walk away, Jake rubbed his face to try and banish the effects of sleep and looked to where Tom had sat during the night.

Gooseflesh sprang up on his arms.

He lost his breath.

His legs shook.

The line of raised rubble ran to where Tom had been sleeping; a livid scar on the terrain whose beginning was hidden by dust clouds.

###

Breathing so hard his lungs felt like they were on fire, Jake finally caught up with Tom. A headache crushed his eyeballs, his head spun, stars sat in his line of sight, and his mouth was so dry his tongue felt like it would crack at any moment.

"Stop!" he finally managed to choke out. After several heavy breaths, he added, "Please?"

Tom stopped and turned to face his friend, occasionally glancing behind as he waited for Jake to catch his breath.

"What happened last night?"

A frown crushed Tom's face, but he didn't reply.

Taking another breath, Jake pointed back to where they'd come from. "I saw the line of rubble."

"What are you talking about?"

"Come on, stop mugging me off. I looked where you were sat and saw the line of lifted rubble that led directly to it."

Tom didn't reply.

"When I was keeping watch the other night something started scrabbling around beneath me."

The frown on Tom's face was replaced by a drawn look of horror.

"Something was toying with me, scratching the stone I was sat on."

"Why didn't you tell me?"

"Are you being serious? I'm not sure if you've noticed or not, but you've been super freaked out since you saw the things chasing me. If I'd told you that—"

"I can't believe you didn't tell me!"

"All right, calm down."

"I won't calm down, Jake. How can I trust you when you keep secrets from me?"

"You're a fine one to fucking talk!"

Standing to his full height, Tom looked down on his friend. "What's that supposed to mean?"

"Secrets, Tom. Like you keeping secrets from me about what's following us."

Folding his arms over his chest, Tom looked over at the Rixon Tower.

"And while I'm being honest, you have to know that it wasn't Rixon who emptied the vending machine."

"What?"

"There was a hole in the bottom of the machine—a hole that had been punched through from the back," Looking into Tom's eyes, he could see his friend was breaking. "...from something underground."

"So you kept that from me too?"

"Would it have helped if I'd told you?"

"It may have prepared me better for last night. How can we survive together if we're dishonest with one another?"

"I'm telling you now, aren't I? Whatever it was had punched its way through the vending machine and climbed up. There were scratches across the red metal as if the thing had sharp claws."

Tom's eyes lost focus as Jake continued.

"There was a line of rubble leading from the machine, to me, and then back to where they'd come from. A line that was exactly the same as the one that led up to where you were sat last night. We're not being followed by Rixon, Tom. I wish we were."

"I bloody know that now, don't I?"

The pair stood in silence for a minute or two before Tom finally turned his back and walked away again.

The burn in Jake's shins wasn't getting any better; wincing with every step, the last few hours had passed in silence. The hill they were currently climbing was getting steeper and the dark sky above was getting darker. They had to reach the summit before they stopped because there was no shelter on the steep incline.

Having lost count of the amount of times he'd tried to get his friend to talk, Jake tried again anyway. "Come on, man. If we're going to find Rory together, we need to be able to communicate."

Tom looked over at him and then dropped his head. "Who am I kidding? We're not going to find Rory." His features twisted like he was about to cry. "If they haven't got him by now, he's probably dead or at the bottom of one of those sinkholes."

Jake was desperate for a rest and he grabbed Tom's forearm to try to make him stop while they talked. Pulling himself away, Tom continued walking.

"Who *are* they, Tom? You're getting the hump with me for not telling you what I saw, but you're doing exactly the same. I'm a big boy, I can handle it."

Tom stopped so abruptly it caught Jake off guard. "No, you can't. Just fucking grow up and accept that you don't need to know."

Stepping closer, Jake snarled. "Don't tell me to grow up. You're the one behaving like a child. You're the one keeping secrets. I want to be prepared for what we might have to face, and you're making that much fucking harder."

Without replying, Tom stared at Jake, his jaw locked tight.

When Jake looked down at Tom's balled right fist, he smiled. "Go on then; do it. Hit me if it'll make you feel better."

Tom continued to stare and clenched his hand so tightly it shook,

Jake stepped back a pace to let the tension in his own body sag before saying, "What are we doing? All we have is each other out here. Let's not fight."

Tom stared for a moment longer, then relaxed and unfurled his fist.

"Just tell me what you saw."

Tom's face buckled and his eyes watered. "It was horrible." Gulping, he continued, "It all happened so quickly. I saw long black claws, white skin, dark mouths but the worst of it was the eyes. Hundreds of pairs of eyes." His own eyes widened. "They all looked straight at me."

Jake let the silence hang for a moment before he finally said, "And?"

Staring into the distance, Tom didn't reply. Eventually, he said, "I don't think I can keep going. I don't think I can do this anymore."

"Don't be ridiculous. You're the strongest man I know. If anyone can do it, it's you."

"Maybe no one can do it."

"Rubbish. Most people would have given up a long time ago, but not you. Not my friend, Tom. You're the only reason I'm alive. I wanted to top myself at several points in the first year, but you and the love you feel for your son has kept me going. Now it's my turn to repay the favour. I'm not going to let you give up."

There was the slightest lift in Tom's posture.

"You never know what's over this next hill."

"Rubble, rubble, and more fucking rubble…" Tom replied.

Laughing, Jake shook his head. "You're probably right, but what if Rory's there too?"

Tom's eyebrows pinched in the middle. "Don't do this to me. I can't take it anymore."

"But he could be. Come on, let's go. We've got a lost boy to find."

A gentle shove encouraged Tom to move as they both started walking again.

It took about twenty minutes to reach the brow of the hill but when Jake got there first and looked over; he turned to his friend and jumped on the spot. "Tom! Tom, come quick!"

***

The tension in her shoulders eased. This world was getting to Tom. Surely he'd give up soon—especially when he saw what Jake was getting excited about…

Chapter Eighteen

Tom was red-faced and out of breath when he reached Jake but hope lifted his features when he asked, "Rory?"

Fuck! Wincing at his friend, Jake remained silent. What could he say to that?

Tom's eyes narrowed, he ground his jaw, and turned a deeper shade of crimson when he looked at the prize in Jake's hand.

Jake offered a tentative smile as he lifted the can. "Peaches! It's a can of peaches."

"I thought you'd found Rory," Tom said as he looked down and his body sagged in disappointment.

"I'm so sorry. I saw the peaches and got excited. I wasn't thinking. Sorry." Jake got to his feet and pointed at a rock. "Sit down, Tom. Rest up while I get this open. You can have the first drink from the juice."

Tom kept his head bowed as he sat down.

Huge lumps of cracked concrete littered the space around the pair; rebar protruding from them at all different angles. Jake watched his friend for a second or two and then pointed at a sheet of red metal. "It's the remains of a car. It's not often that we see cars now. Most of them are buried a good few metres below us. This must have been a multi-storey car park or something."

When Tom didn't reply, Jake scratched his head and busied himself with opening the can.

Jake looked at the ring-pull with doubt and then looked at his twisted and gnarled hands. The past few years had turned them into old roots not capable of once-simple chores.

Gritting his jaw helped him concentrate and block out the pain that nestled in his knuckles. Jake slipped a long fingernail beneath the ring-pull and lifted it.

"Argh!" White-hot pain tore through his hand.

Tom leapt up and frowned at his friend. "What's up? Are you okay?"

The nail on Jake's finger had snapped far too low and blood was leaking over the top of it. Biting down on his bottom lip, he looked at Tom. "I just snapped my fucking fingernail."

Raising an eyebrow, Tom looked Jake up and down before sitting back down and letting his long body slump once again.

Trying to be more cautious this time, he used the nail on his middle finger to tease the ring pull away from the can. As he lifted it to the point where it was just about the pierce the lid, the ring-pull snapped off. Holding it in a pinch, he looked at it for a minute before glancing over at Tom.

Tom shook his head.

Jake held the can up and glared at it. "You're not beating me. Not today!" Throwing it up and catching it again, he looked around.

Dashing it against the concrete seemed like the best option. Raising it above his head, Jake suddenly stopped as his eyes fell on a piece of rebar that protruded from the ground like a spear. *Perfect.*

Jake stepped closer to it and lifted the can again. As he brought it crashing down, he heard Tom shout, "Noooooooooooo!"

It was too late.

***

Pulling her knees to her chest, she slapped her hand across her mouth to stifle her scream.

Chapter Nineteen

White-hot pain exploded in Jake's palm, and he roared at the sky, "Arghhhhhh!" Queasiness sat in his guts as he looked down at his hand impaled on the piece of rebar.

Tom rushed over and grabbed Jake's chin to lift his head up. "Just look at me. Don't look down, okay?"

Nodding, Jake bit his bottom lip, but he couldn't help glancing at his hand. The pole it was impaled on had already turned slick with his blood.

Pulling Jake's chin up again, Tom snarled, "I said look at me!"

With fire stretching up his forearm like poison was getting into his veins, Jake's voice shook, "I'm scared, Tom."

Wrapping both hands around Jake's wrist, Tom shook his head. "Don't be. It'll be fine, just keep looking at me." Without warning, Tom yanked Jake's hand free.

The wet squelch ran directly to Jake's knees, and if it wasn't for Tom grabbing him, he'd have dropped like a wet sandbag. When Jake turned his hand over, it looked like stigmata.

Instead of helping him, Tom rescued the bloody can and wrapped his lips around it as he chugged the peach juice. Pulling it away with a satisfied gasp, Tom burped several times, and then handed the can to Jake. "Drink it, we can't waste the juice."

Taking it with his good hand, Jake drank what was left, his gag reflex desperately trying to reject the sweet and metallic liquid.

It ran out too quickly, and once he'd finished, Jake looked at his hand again. It was hard to see the extent of the damage, but fortunately the pole hadn't passed all the way through. It belched thick and syrupy blood in time with his pulse and with each surge of claret, his hand throbbed.

As blood leaked from the wound and soaked the rocks at his feet, Jake was overcome with dizziness. Looking at Tom, he opened his mouth to call for help, but before he could speak, his legs gave way beneath him and his world went black.

Jake opened his eyes and coughed at the same time, then saw a blur of someone leaning over him. Shouting out, he tried to sit up, but his injured hand gave way beneath him.

As he crashed back down against the rubble, Jake crossed his arms in front of his face and cowered behind them. "Please, don't kill me. Please."

The thing grabbed him and he tried to twist away from it until he heard Tom's voice.

"Jake, it's me! It's okay. I'm here, mate, there's nothing to worry about."

Jake let Tom help him sit upright to catch his breath and waited for Tom to come into focus. Despite the peach juice, his throat was so dry his word came out as a croak. "Tom?"

"Shh, Jake, I'm here, everything's fine."

"How long have you been sitting there?"

Tom rubbed his face and cleared his throat. "For as long as you've been passed out."

His friend's eyes were bloodshot; stress and exhaustion had left trails on his face. Jake gulped. "Thank you for looking after me."

Despite the thick throb running through his hand, Jake was surprised to see it look reasonably normal. Other than being tightly bound by a dirty and now bloody rag, it looked exactly as it had before he'd skewered it. He'd expected it to be as big as a football.

Scanning the grey sky, Jake frowned. "How long have I been out?"

"A few hours."

Jake sat up farther and waited for everything to settle around him as he rode the nauseating wave surging through his guts.

When he finally felt normal again, he picked up the punctured can, his dried blood still on it, and peered inside. Although the can was old and battered, the contents looked brand new.

Jake retrieved one of the slippery peach slices, lifted his scarf, and slipped it into his mouth. The slimy piece of fruit, pregnant with juice, sat on his tongue. When he bit down on it, it released a sweet shot of liquid and Jake groaned. Turning to Tom, Jake held the can in his direction.

Tom quickly snatched a peach slice for himself and swallowed it whole. A slight grin lifted one side of his mouth. "Oh my god! That's amazing!"

Jake took another piece and smiled at his friend. "Thanks again for looking out for me, Tom. I say it a lot, but I don't know what I'd do without you around."

When Jake bit the next piece of fruit, he looked over to the rebar he'd speared his hand on and his blood turned cold. "Tom."

"Yeah?"

"You say I was out for a few hours?"

"Well, maybe a little bit longer than a few hours."

Keeping his eyes on the pole, Jake scratched his face. "How much longer?"

"About a day."

"So you slept while you were waiting for me?"

"Yeah. I had to. I'm as knackered as you are. I had to get some rest."

"Did you hear anything in the night?"

"No. Why?"

With a shaky hand, Jake pointed at the rebar. "There's no blood left on the pole."

Realisation dawned on Tom's face as he stared at the pole and gulped. "There's no blood on the rocks around it either."

Turning his attention to the rebar again, Jake then noticed the line of raised rubble leading away from it.

Speaking in no more than a whisper, Tom said, "They're getting braver, Jake."

***

Opening and closing her hand as if Jake's pain was her own, she watched the pair. Jake was becoming more observant. Maybe he'd become aware enough to save his own life.

Chapter Twenty

Jake kept his eyes down as they walked and listened to the shifting rubble and howling wind.

"I've had enough, Jake."

Jake stopped and turned to his friend. "What do you mean?"

"Don't do this to me."

"Do what?"

"You know what."

When Jake looked at Tom properly—his sunken grey eyes, his ratty beard, his pale skin—a pang of grief gripped his heart. *When did he get so old?*

"I've had enough of this life; of scavenging like animals." Tom looked away and pointed at a fox walking over the ruined landscape. "Hell, even the animals are doing better than us. We've been living like this for *years* now."

Jake put his good hand on Tom's emaciated shoulder, the sharpness of it made him want to withdraw. "But we've come so far."

"Have we? Really? What have we done? We live like tramps, hoping that we'll find some old scrap of food, some sort of shelter, some… anything."

Shaking his head, Jake looked around. "It won't be long before things start growing again. Nature will beat this."

"You've been saying that since Rixon destroyed our city. Every day we look for signs of life, but there aren't any. This place is sterile. The only way to survive is to put a headset on." Tom said as he battled the wind to retie his ponytail yet again.

"They want you to think New Reality's the only option, but life cycles; things *have* to change—you can't stop nature." Staring into the distance, Jake's eyes lost focus. "It will always win out."

"We all have our own reality, right?"

Ignoring the question, Jake raised his eyebrows. "I'm sure you just need a rest."

"I need more than a rest."

Jake didn't reply.

"The only reality we have in this world is our own, right? The life I perceive and live is my truth."

A particularly nasty twinge ran through Jake's hand as he nodded.

"We see the world through our own eyes. Experience it through our own senses."

"What about the shared reality we experience from interacting with one another?" Jake asked.

"We still experience that through our own receptors and our own viewpoint, regardless of whether it's shared or not. It's only real because I perceive it as real. Everything is subjective. If I plug into the game and experience a new reality, then why can't I choose to accept that as my truth?"

Jake looked away and caught a glimpse of the first gamer he'd seen in days. Dragging Tom over to him, Jake kicked the man as hard as he could. It felt like kicking a crash mat and it aggravated the sharp pain in his right shin. "Look at it, Tom," he said, purposefully omitting a gender. "You want to be like that? Inanimate? Stupid? Is that the existence you want? Is that the reality you'd choose?"

"Look at us; we're walking skeletons that look like we'll snap at any moment. At least he's well fed," Tom countered.

"He's a slug."

"In our reality he is, but not in his. He's probably relaxing on a beach while a beautiful woman oils him down. He probably looks like a movie star in his world. Isn't that all that matters?"

Another burning wave gripped Jake's palm. Pulling air through his gritted teeth, he shook his head. "But it's not real."

"What is, Jake? Look around. We live like cockroaches in a world where Rixon is God. We have no food. No shelter. No women. If this is living, I'd rather play New Reality; I'd rather create my own destiny."

"But New Reality can't give us the social interactions that are so important to us as people. Don't you believe in an interconnected collective consciousness?"

Tom sighed. "I'm a scientist, Jake, I don't believe in the same things as you."

"But how do you know it works? How do you know the headset will respond to your desires?" Lifting his scarf, Jake spat grit from his mouth. "What if it responds to your nightmares? What if you feel trapped and can't escape? You can't take the headset off again because you won't know you have it on." Imploring his friend with raised palms, the action throwing another sharp sting through his wounded hand, Jake lifted his eyebrows. "So how can you know, Tom? How?"

"How do *you* know everything will work out fine if I stay here?"

"Faith."

"In what? Rixon?"

"No; faith in me and that I can carry on until things change."

"What about your teeth?"

"What about them?"

"The toothache that's growing at the back of your mouth."

Running his tongue over his back teeth, Jake flinched at the jagged pain. "They'll be okay."

"Have you ever had toothache? It's like your brain's melting. What will you do with no painkillers? That's if

139

you don't die of thirst before that." Tom glanced behind them.

"I get it now."

"What?"

"It's about them, isn't it? The things following us. Everything's about them."

Looking from side to side, Tom shook his head. "No."

"Really?"

"Okay, it is a little bit about them." Pointing at his chest and leaning forwards, Tom opened his eyes wide. "I've seen them, Jake. I know what's following us."

"And you *still* won't tell me. Do you realise just how tedious it's getting?"

"It's because I don't want to remember what they look like. To talk about them is to keep them alive in my head."

"What about Rory? Who will save him?"

A twitch pulled Tom's face, and his words lacked the assertion of those before them. "Maybe he's better off. Look around, why would I want to bring him back into this world?"

"Because it's real and you want to make sure that he's okay, don't you?" It was an underhanded tactic, but Jake was desperate.

Tom turned his back on Jake and stared at the tower in the distance. After a few seconds, he spun around again with his index finger raised. "One week. Seven days is all I'm going to give it. If we haven't found Rory by then, I'm giving up."

Shoving his bandaged hand in Tom's direction, Jake beamed a smile at him. "Deal."

Staring at the bloody mess, Tom sneered like he'd rather shake a land mine.

***

She ground her jaw as she watched the interaction. Why didn't Jake let him go? It would make everything less complicated. Her patience wouldn't last another week. Something had to change to speed up the process. If it didn't, she was going to have to intervene.

Chapter Twenty-One

"Tom!" Jake called.

When he looked up to see Tom was still walking although Jake had stopped, he tried again. "Tom!"

Tom spun around, threw his hands up in the air, and shouted, "What?"

Pointing, Jake said, "Look."

Jake chose to ignore Tom's sigh as his friend walked back over to him. "What is it?"

Pointing again, he watched Tom's eyes follow his direction. When Tom looked back up, his expression was stony. "A chimney. So what?"

"But what does a chimney mean?"

"It means that at some point, probably a long time ago, it allowed someone to have a fire indoors," Tom answered sarcastically.

"Exactly! Do you think there's a house beneath us?"

"There are probably many houses beneath us. Why would I care?"

An involuntary groan escaped Jake as another sharp pain ran through his hand. "The house it's attached to might still be intact. It'd be nice to see something else has hung on during this clusterfuck, don't you think? Something other than us."

"You think we're hanging on?" Looking Jake up and down, Tom shook his head. "Besides, it's only a house. I've seen plenty of houses in my time."

"I've seen plenty of roast chickens, but that doesn't mean I wouldn't piss myself if we came across one right now."

"That's different, Jake."

Without replying, Jake pulled his hair from his face and peered into the darkness. The chimney still smelt of smoke. "Imagine if we could see what was going on down there."

"Jesus, Jake! Have you lost your fucking mind? If there's anything down there, I really don't want to see it. Seeing those… *things* once is enough for me."

Every time Jake watched Tom retreat into the dark memory, anxious anticipation gnawed away at his insides. "I've not seen them yet."

"You don't want to."

"Can't I be the judge of that?"

"With all due respect, Jake, I'm not sure you can." Turning his index finger against his chest, Tom poked himself. "I've seen them. I have the nightmares to prove it. This existence is hard enough without the thought of those things in your mind."

Softening his tone, Jake said, "Please, I need to see what's following us. I need to be prepared for what may come. It's worse not knowing. It's like watching a horror film before you've seen the monster. That's the scariest part. Besides, what if there's food down there? Water maybe."

Although the scarf covered his mouth, Jake could see Tom was chewing his lips. "There's nothing down there but darkness and nightmares."

"Dare to dream, Tom. They may manifest as something real one day."

"Dreams don't exist here," Tom said.

"Dreams exist everywhere. In the darkest hours, dreams burn brighter than ever. Without dreams, we have nothing."

"Without dreams, we have logic and well-realised plans. Hope only leads to disappointment."

"Well, aren't you cheery today?"

Pulling his shoulders back, Tom stood up to his full height. "Look, I don't want to be here anymore. Remember? I'm hanging on because of you—"

"And Rory."

The fury left Tom and his eyes glazed. "I'm finding it hard to believe that Rory's still about. I'm giving *you* this extra week, Jake."

Jake dropped his voice to a whisper. "Thank you for everything you've done for me, Tom. I truly appreciate it. You're right, I can't know the impact that seeing the monsters has had on you, but please let me try and see them for myself. In a week's time, I'll be on my own and I need to know what I'm up against."

Jake walked over to the chimney and peered down into the darkness again.

Tom scowled at Jake for a moment and then looked up at the sky.

"What are you doing, Tom?"

Scratching his chin, Tom continued staring at the clouds. "The sun is directly above us."

Jake shrugged. "How can you tell?"

"Find the darkest part of the sky on all four sides and you can roughly work out where the sun is. The change in light is subtle, but if you have any chance of seeing down the chimney, it'll be now."

Tom hunched down and picked up a piece of metal no bigger than a sheet of paper. Dusting it off, he handed the shiny sheet to his friend. "Try this. Although I think you'll be disappointed. The house probably caved in years ago."

Pain tore through his damaged hand as he gripped the cold metal tightly and tried to prevent the wind from ripping it from his clutches. Jake nodded. "Thank you. You're a genius."

Jake dropped the metal down the chimney and watched it fall. It turned end over end like an autumn leaf before hitting the ground with a light clang and landing at the perfect angle pointing into the darkness. Whooping Jake punched the air. When he looked up at Tom, he saw his friend staring at him and shaking his head.

"What?"

"You just dropped it in there!"

"And?"

"You could have tried to place it."

Jake stood back and pointed down the chimney. "But it worked perfectly. Look."

Tom shook his head again. "No thanks."

Jake leaned over the chimney, drew a deep breath as his heart galloped, and called out, "Hello?"

Jake tensed in anticipation of a reply as his voice dove into the darkness.

There was none.

When he looked up at Tom, the big man pointed in the direction they were heading and said, "Right, there's nothing there. Can we go now?"

Dropping his shoulders in resignation, Jake was just about to move on when he heard a noise coming from the bottom of the chimney. When he looked over and saw Tom's eyes wide with fear, he knew that he'd heard it too.

**

The noise of her shifting went off like a bomb in the silence. Remaining perfectly still, she held her breath and waited.

She couldn't see a thing when she stared at the makeshift mirror. Squinting, she looked harder and moved forwards slightly.

Blinking against the burn in her eyes, she sat and waited. Jake was going to look down again. He was going to find out what was below. He couldn't resist it.

Chapter Twenty-Two

Jake focused on the chimney and heard Tom growl, "Don't, Jake. Don't be stupid."

The scrabbling turned into a clicking like bony fingers tapping on glass.

"Jake! What are you doing?"

With his body tense and his stomach tight, Jake stepped towards the noise and peered in.

Swallowing a gulp of the smoke-scented air, Jake jumped when the darkness shifted.

Seconds later, there was a long and slow scratching sound that ran goose bumps down his spine. It was the same scratch that had tormented him beneath the gravestone.

"Come on, Jake, you don't need to see this. Let's go."

But Jake couldn't move. Pushing his face so far into the chimney he could taste the old fires, Jake listened for anything other than his quickening breath in the cavernous space. He shifted to the side to let more of the overhead light in so he could see better.

Despite the tiredness and pain, his twitching legs were preparing to run—but only after he'd seen what was down there. Watching the darkness in the reflective metal, Jake shivered from the adrenaline running through him.

A high-pitched and tormented scream swelled at the bottom before flying up the chimney. Jake pulled his head away and stumbled backwards as if the sound had dealt him a physical blow.

His bony bottom landed on the jagged ground with a nauseating crack. Jake forgot himself and tried to push himself up with his damaged hand; searing pain tore through his palm. Taking deep breaths, he used his good left hand to get upright.

Moving with a stilted gait because of his aching coccyx, Jake glanced at Tom. Although the tall man shook his head at him, Jake ignored his warning and looked into the chimney again.

The scrabbling sounds were now accompanied by throaty breaths. Deep and resonating in the cavernous space below, they were the sound of a large beast.

Shuddering, Jake remained where he was. He had to see what was down there. When else would he get the chance?

Clearing his throat sent an echo into the house below. "Hello?" Jake drew a breath to speak again then froze as the reflected shadows at the bottom of the chimney suddenly shifted. A pebble skipped across a stone floor followed by a glass bottle falling over.

Then he saw a shape. A flash of skin, as white as chalk and black hair, matted with grease. Eyes…

Oh, my god.

Jake shook and his breath quickened.

The eyes were red as if covered with a film of blood and they stared into the makeshift mirror. They stared straight at him.

Then, as quickly as it had appeared, it was gone. All that was left was the reflection of its dark domain.

Turning to Tom, his teeth chattering, Jake couldn't find the words.

Tom's eyebrows pinched in the middle. "Have you seen enough?"

All Jake managed was a febrile nod.

Tom walked over to the chimney and grunted as he lifted a large rock and dropped it down the hole. It hit the ground with a loud thud and the clattering of metal.

A hissing scream responded.

Tom grabbed Jake's shoulder and said, "Come on, mate, let's get moving."

***

She pulled away, sat in the darkness, and scratched her face with her long nails. If they thought a rock dropped down a chimney was enough to stop her, they were seriously mistaken.

Now that Jake had seen her, surely this would be the unraveling she'd been waiting for?

Chapter Twenty-Three

The whir of the Bot's mini blade snapped Jake's shoulders tight and his eyes widened. Backing away, Jake looked at his immobile friend. "Tom, we've got to leave… now!"

But Tom wasn't moving. Frozen to the spot, he stared down at the wide eyes of his dead wife.

Anxious energy buzzed in Jake's legs as the whir got louder. It was moving fast, but he couldn't see it yet because of the dust on the wind. Looking up the hill at his exit, he stamped his foot. "Come on! This isn't the time to hang around."

The tall man seemed to have no awareness of the Bot. The rock his wife had hit her head against was slick with blood. The headset they'd just removed sat discarded and rocking in the gales.

Jake bit down on his bottom lip and looked in the direction of the whir.

Then it burst through the murky sky. The black Bot was huge, its torso as big as Tom's. Shouting burned Jake's grit-damaged throat. "We need to go! Hurry up, man!"

When Tom still didn't move, Jake gritted his teeth. "Argh!" Running back down the slope towards his friend, Jake rode the shifting ground.

With one eye on the Bot, he grabbed Tom's skinny arm and yanked hard.

Jake misjudged the tall man's resistance and pulled with such force that he fell backwards and dragged Tom down on top of him.

Landing over a large lump of concrete sent a nauseating crack through Jake's back and white light flashed through his vision. Battling his wheezing lungs, Jake watched Tom get to his feet.

A deep frown crushed Tom's face. "What the hell are you doing? What's wrong with you?"

Still fighting for breath, Jake pointed in the direction of the Bot. It was only about thirty metres away now.

Tom's eyes widened as he looked between Jake and their attacker. "Fuck!" he yelled and took off running.

Temporarily paralysed from the fall, Jake watched his friend disappear in the opposite direction. If he'd had the lung capacity, he'd have called after him. What was he doing?

Tom ran at the Bot.

What the fuck?

When the tall man grabbed the discarded headset, Jake suddenly understood.

Running away again, Tom waved it at the Bot. "Oi, you. Over here."

As he scrambled up a small hill, Jake winced. The Bot was gaining on him. Jake forced himself up, his breathing ragged, *and began his hobbled ascent to safety. When he looked back over to where Tom was, he saw the headset had been left and his friend had vanished.*

He sped up as he got close to the top of the hill; the whir of the Bot's mini helicopter blade spurring him on. He looked around and saw a claw extend from the bottom of the Bot. It hooked around the headset and then the Bot turned to face Jake.

"Fuck!"

Hearing the whine of the Bot's Gatling guns starting up, Jake turned and ran.

Chips of bricks, concrete and glass sprayed his back as the ground received a peppering of bullets. Each piece stung like a snake bite. Once he reached the summit of the hill, an explosion of searing pain smashed into the triceps on his left arm. Spinning like a top, he saw a splash of blood punched into the air. Then he saw the Bot. The ends of the Gatling gun's barrels were red-hot circles.

Maintaining his momentum, he fell backwards over the brow of the hill.

###

Jake's eyes flashed open and all he saw was darkness above him. With his heart pounding and his hand stinging, he groaned. How many times would he have to dream about killing Tom's wife?

Jake stayed still and listened to see if he could hear anything over the loud wind. As his eyes adjusted to the night, he could just make out the hazy red glow coming from the letters on the Rixon Tower. It was never truly dark anymore.

Sitting up slowly, his hand feeling like it was leaking poison into his veins; he looked over at his friend. Tom had his head bowed and was cradling his knees.

He had promised Jake one week. A day had passed, and all they'd found was more problems.

Once he was upright, his legs aching, his hand still throbbing, Jake walked over to his friend.

Hunched like an old vulture, Tom looked up and Jake nodded at him.

Squinting against the grit, Tom nodded back. "Are you okay?"

Shrugging, Jake sat down next to his friend. Staring into the night, he said, "Have you slept at all?"

Tom shivered and shook his head. "No."

Not knowing what to say, Jake remained silent.

"Bad dream?" Tom asked.

Nodding, Jake stared at the faint glow of the Rixon Tower.

"About the things following us?"

Jake shook his head.

"Thalia?"

"Yep," he replied tersely.

"Me too," Tom sighed. "I dream about her every night. It's like life's playing a cruel trick on me. Every time I go to sleep, I'm plagued with the memory of killing my wife. Whenever I'm awake, it's the memory of those things."

Not knowing if he wanted an answer, Jake swallowed a dusty gulp of air and asked, "Have you heard anything tonight?"

With a half-smile on his face, Tom raised an eyebrow. "Other than you whimpering like a bitch in your sleep?"

Lifting his middle finger at him, Jake scoffed, "Fuck you!"

Tom's smile fell from his face and he stared into the distance.

Tom eventually broke the silence. "I bet the arseholes in the tower are having a good laugh at our expense. It must be entertaining for them if nothing else."

Before Jake could respond, Tom sighed and ran a hand through his hair. "I can't believe we left them in the first place. What kind of a husband and father was I to leave my wife and son alone in this world?"

"Don't you dare say that, Tom. You were trying to find a way to get their headsets off."

Grinding his jaw, Tom's voice cracked. "I left them on their own for over a year. What kind of a man leaves his wife and kid lying in shit for a year?"

"You left them when the city was fine. Once it had been destroyed, it was impossible to find anything anymore. There were no landmarks left. It was like trying to find an ant in the Sahara."

"To make things worse, we returned with nothing. No way of removing the headsets. No way of saving them. It was a waste of time, Jake. It was a year-long wild goose chase that ended with the death of my wife."

"We tried our best."

"We killed her, Jake."

Throwing his left arm over Tom's shoulder, Jake said, "Come on, man, don't do this to yourself."

The deep red glow from the Rixon Tower caught the shiny trails on Tom's cheeks. Gulping, his large Adam's apple dipping on his long neck, Tom lifted his right arm across his chest and held Jake's left hand.

Feeling the calloused grip of his friend's long fingers, Jake pulled him in tight and held him as he cried for his dead wife.

***

When was Jake going to accept that Tom didn't want to be on this planet anymore? If he got that through his thick head, then maybe he'd have a chance. She didn't want to kill Jake but he wasn't giving her much choice at the moment.

As she watched the pair fall asleep, she sighed. A week wasn't long when she thought about the time she'd been following the pair for, but the final sprint was always the hardest. Maybe she should just do something about it now. They were sleeping after all.

Sitting up straight, she stretched the aches from her body and took a deep breath.

Action needed to be taken. She was bored with waiting.

Chapter Twenty-Four

The second Jake woke up his mind went to the deep throb in his palm. It was a constant that could only be avoided with sleep. Looking across at Tom, who was already awake, he lifted his bandaged hand. "Do you think it'll get any worse?"

Tom looked away and squinted into the wind.

"Tom? Do you—"

"I heard you, Jake." Scratching his beard, Tom shook his head. "I was choosing not to answer."

Jake's heart fluttered. "You think it's that bad?"

When Tom looked at him, his grey eyes pinched ever so slightly.

Taking a deep breath, Jake exhaled hard. "How long do you think I've got before it's life-threatening?"

Tom didn't reply.

Looking at his hand for a moment longer, Jake attempted to make a fist and winced. After resting it on his knee, he looked up at the sky. It had changed from black to grey—night had become day. When he turned to Tom again, the wind blew into his face and grit pattered the lenses of his glasses. "Have you been awake long?"

Shrugging, Tom said, "Not really; half an hour maybe."

Silence surrounded the pair again as Jake watched Tom stare at the fuzzy glow of the Rixon Tower in the distance.

Kicking a stone in front of him, Tom sighed. "I'm not sure I can do a week, Jake."

A pain ran through Jake's chest, and his voice turned whiny. "Come on, Tom, you promised me."

"I know I did. But I just don't know if I can do this anymore."

Jake's anger passed when he looked at Tom's exhausted face and drawn features. Heavy bags hung beneath his eyes and his breathing was shallow. He was done.

Shaking his head, Jake said, "No."

Tom looked up and raised an eyebrow. "No?"

Jake got to his feet and held his left hand out. "I'm not letting you give up, Tom."

The tall man didn't move.

"Don't give me that puppy-dog stare. Get up, now! You owe me the week you promised me. You owe Rory the week you promised me."

Tom's face buckled before he took Jake's offered hand and got to his feet. "Why do you use Rory to keep me going?"

Losing his patience, Jake raised his voice. "Because that's why we're out here, isn't it? That's why we've been walking in fucking circles for the past few years."

"Don't shout at me."

"Stop being a prick then, Tom."

Drawing a sharp intake of breath, Tom's brow furrowed.

"I'm sorry. It's just... I feel like I've put my plans on hold for the past few years and now you want to give up? I could have been looking for signs of the beautiful planet we lived on years ago but I stayed with you in Birmingham to look for your wife and son."

When Tom didn't reply, Jake continued, "I want the past few years to have counted for something."

With a slumped frame, Tom looked at his friend. "Sometimes the wisdom is in knowing when to quit."

Balling his left fist, Jake's tense arm shook. When Tom remained limp and dejected, Jake grabbed him. "You owe me six more days."

Tom suddenly froze as he stared past Jake. What little colour he had in his face drained from it instantly. Even with the rag on, Jake saw his jaw working as if he were trying to speak.

"What is it, Tom?"

While rubbing his forehead, Tom turned on the spot while looking at the ground surrounding them.

Jake mimicked Tom's spinning until they faced each other again. Staring into Tom's wide eyes, Jake said, "What does it mean?"

When Tom didn't reply, Jake looked around again. At first, all he saw was a chaotic mess of raised lines of rubble. They ran a crisscross pattern all about them like the random burrowing of some insane creature. Looking from one line to the next, Jake's head flicked from side to side.

After a moment longer of scanning the ground, the snapshots of disorder suddenly came together and his skin turned to gooseflesh. Double-checking to make sure he wasn't imagining it, he started to shake.

They were in the centre of a five-pointed star within a circle. The things must have done it while they slept. Jake continued to look at the perfectly formed shape. He swallowed a dry gulp, and spoke from the side of his mouth in a whisper, "Can you see what it is, Tom?"

When there was no reply, Jake looked across at his pale friend. "Can you see what it is, Tom?"

Nodding, the tall man said, "Yep."

"What the fuck is it?"

Tom rubbed his temple with a shaking hand. "A pentagram."

"A pentagram?"

Tom's eyes were glazed as if he'd retreated into his mind. "It's a spiritual symbol."

Not sure he wanted the answer, Jake lifted a shrug. "A good one?"

"Depends."

"On what?"

"On whether it's pointing up or down. Down is for the devil."

Just the thought of the question turned Jake's blood cold. "And which way is it pointing?"

Nodding at the symbols on either side of them, Jake suddenly saw what they were when Tom said, "Well, by looking at those pitch forks, I'd say it was pointing down."

Before Jake could reply, Tom had set off, avoiding the lines of rubble like he was running an army assault course.

Looking around and picking an equally cautious path through the symbol, Jake lifted his legs high as if something were nipping at his heels and followed his friend.

***

It didn't matter how far or fast they ran away. They weren't getting away.

Chapter Twenty-Five

The pair had been walking all day and all Jake could think about was the pentagram. When Tom moved over to a pile of rubble, Jake stopped. "What is it?"

As Tom pulled lumps of concrete and debris away, Jake walked over to stand next to him. With his damaged hand, he didn't try to help.

The more hard-core Tom pulled away, the quicker he started clearing a hole. Then Jake saw it—a small, round piece of blue plastic. When Tom grabbed it, it crackled as he wiggled it free.

Looking at Tom's prize, Jake swallowed an arid gulp. "Water."

Tom broke the seal on the large bottle and handed it to Jake to drink first.

Lifting it up to what little light there was in the sky, the clear liquid seemingly uncontaminated. Jake looked back at his friend. "You're letting me have it first? Shouldn't you go first? You found it."

"Stop being soft, Jake. Just take a bloody sip."

When Jake lifted the bottle to his lips, the cool liquid filled his mouth. Although his body craved the quench of the water, he took a small taste and passed it back. "Slow and steady so we don't throw it up."

Watching his friend drink, phlegm sticking in his throat, Jake couldn't take the bottle back quickly enough when Tom returned it.

After they were done, the water swilling in Jake's guts, he sat down on a nearby rock and looked at his hand. "You didn't answer me before, Tom."

"About what?"

"How long have I got before my hand turns septic? Seriously, how long would you give it?"

"I don't know, Jake. Maybe your body will fight against the infection and you'll be all right."

"You don't sound sure."

"I'm not. I just don't know. I'm sorry."

Looking at the dirty bandages wrapping his hands, Jake sighed.

With the conversation dying, Jake sat on his rock and looked at what little he could see around him. When his eyes caught some movement on the brow of a small ridge, his heart jumped. Staring at it for a moment longer, he saw that his eyes weren't deceiving him. The ground was lifting up slowly as if something was crawling beneath it.

Standing up, Jake stretched to the sky and, trying to be as casual as possible, said, "Okay, I'm ready to set off again."

Frowning up at him, Tom remained seated, his long body folded over in a slump. "I thought you wanted a rest?"

"I do. I did. I'm fine now. That water's worked wonders."

When Tom looked down at the ground, Jake glanced over at the raising rubble again. It was still lifting, slowly crawling towards them. "Come on, man. If we've only got a few days left together, we may as well cover as much ground as possible."

Tom stood up with a long groan. The heavy wind rocked the tall man where he stood. "You're so bloody contrary, Jake."

Raising his eyebrows, Jake simply shrugged. "Come on, let's go."

Moving as if every joint ached, Tom took Jake's lead and followed him directly away from the thing. With the memory of the bloody eyes sat in his mind, Jake powered up the next hill and waited at the top for his friend.

Tom reached the top a minute or so later and red-faced from the effort, shook his head and continued ahead of Jake down the other side.

Just before Jake followed him, he looked back. The raised line of rubble suddenly closed the gap between them at a sprint and Jake flinched when it stopped just metres away from him; rocks and debris spraying up as it halted.

Jake stared at it for a moment, his heart beating in his neck, and waited to see if it would move again. When it didn't, he spun around and headed after Tom.

As Jake stared at the slim back of his tall friend, his mouth dried and his stomach was gripped tight. No matter how fast they travelled, the thing was quicker. The only reason it hadn't caught them was because it had chosen not to.

It was toying with them.

***

Why was he protecting Tom? She didn't want to kill Jake, despite her orders, but he was making it hard for her. Why didn't he just let the tall idiot go?

Five days was too long. It couldn't go on like this. With shot nerves and a stabbing headache, she rubbed her face.

Five days was far too long.

Chapter Twenty-Six

Whenever Jake looked around, he saw the rubble following them. It lurked in the dust storm, just at the edge of his vision. Was that why Tom hadn't seen it? Maybe the sunglasses offered Jake a longer line of sight. No matter the reason, he wasn't about to tell Tom. The last thing his maudlin friend needed was another excuse to put on a headset.

Trying to stay positive, Jake turned to Tom as they climbed the next hill. "This is it. When we get to the top of this hill, we're going to see a forest stretching out before us. No more bricks and rubble and twisted metal. We're going to see lush greenery filling the distance."

Jake held his breath and took the last step to the top of the hill.

Releasing a long and deflating sigh, he shook his head as he looked below him. Lying in the next crater was more rubble, more bricks, and more twisted metal. Although this time, stretched across their path was a huge electricity pylon that covered the ground like the skeleton of a dinosaur.

When Tom appeared next to him, he looked down and then raised an eyebrow at Jake.

Jake looked back at the pylon and watched a mangy fox with a gammy back leg winding in and out of the metal structure. In this world of scavengers, he was no better than the flea-bitten canid. Even the concept of a food chain was now obsolete. Other than gamers, all that was left were scavengers and the dead—he looked back at the raised rubble again—and then there were the things.

The strong winds prevented the fox from detecting their presence. Jake put a finger to his veiled lips, bent down, and grabbed a small rock. With his stomach rumbling, he allowed the weight of it to settle in the palm of his left hand. Jake paused for a moment as he visualised the rock connecting with the fox's head and then pulled his arm back and hurled it.

The clang of the rock hitting the electricity pylon made the fox look up, its ears pricked. For the briefest moment, Jake and the fox stared at each other. The golden eyes of the mangy creature were wide but not petrified. It was almost as if the fox scoffed at the threat posed to him by these two weak men. The fox then jogged away from them in the opposite direction.

When Jake turned around, he saw Tom looking at him.

"That was close, Jake."

"All right."

"I'm being serious. The fox only needed to be about thirty times its size and you'd have scored a bull's eye. Well done."

Glaring at Tom, Jake showed him his raised middle finger.

Tom shielded his brow, scanned the horizon, and said, "The view from every hill looks exactly the same. More concrete, more rubble, more metal."

"That's why I'm going to leave this crap city when I get the chance. There has to be something else out there."

"You hope."

"All right, Tom. I know you're ready to go, but there's no need to piss on my fireworks. In five days' time, you can have your wish. Until then, give me some happy memories to keep me going, yeah?"

Shaking his head, Jake then said, "Come on, let's keep moving." Patting Tom on the back, a little harder than he hoped because he had less control over his weaker left hand, Jake's stomach sank as he watched his friend stumble.

Everything moved in slow motion. First Tom wobbled, his arms wind milling; then he took several steps down the hill, each one longer than the last, each one less stable. When his legs crumpled beneath him, his body headed towards the bottom of the hill faster than Tom could control.

Jake winced as Tom connected hard with the pylon— then cringed when he heard a loud crack followed by a throat-tearing scream.

***

Surely this was it. There was no way he was getting up from that. Rubbing her hands together, she closed her sore eyes and whispered, "Please let this be the end of him. Jake deserves a chance without me having to kill him. Please give up, Tom. Please."

Chapter Twenty-Seven

Jake rushed down the hill, riding the landslide as best he could, and skidded to a halt next to his best friend. "Shit, Tom! Are you okay? I'm so sorry."

Tom's usually pallid face was purple. Clenching his jaw, he clung onto his hip and screamed through his gritted teeth.

Jake could feel his lungs tightening as he anxiously gasped, "Tom, what's going on, man? Are you okay? Talk to me."

Taking heavy breaths, Tom forced his words out, grunting between each one. "Does… It… Look… Like," When he paused, his facial muscles writhed like a bag of snakes. "…I'm okay?"

Looking Tom up and down as if searching his form would reveal how to fix his friend, Jake's eyes stopped on Tom's hip and the hand holding it. It was yet another question that he didn't want an answer to. "It's broken, isn't it?"

A strange calm came over Tom as he grunted and lowered his eyes. "I think so, yes."

Jake leaned over, wiped the thick hair away from Tom's sweating brow, and offered a single, ineffective word. "Sorry."

***

She wasn't sorry. She was about as far from sorry as she could be. Watching Tom as he lay there fighting against his pain, she leaned back and relaxed.

"At last!"

Chapter Twenty-Eight

To stand by and watch his friend writhing on the floor as if he were possessed was hard enough for Jake... knowing that he was the reason for his pain was torture. Holding Tom's large and bony hand, he watched him contort in ways he thought were beyond the physical capabilities of the exhausted man.

Other than an apology, Jake had nothing to offer. Sat next to his friend, occasionally mopping sweat off his face and offering words of comfort, he watched Tom slip into states of delirium that he wasn't sure he'd ever pull out of.

All the while, the raised line of rubble moved steadily closer with each passing hour.

Hours passed and all Tom could do was groan and writhe while his eyes rolled in his head. When they suddenly focused, Jake jumped. The stark lucidity staring up at him made his spine tingle.

Speaking in a pitch that was somewhere between a growl and a cough Tom said, "It hurts so much."

Jake pushed Tom's hair away from his face, leaned over, and said, "It'll be okay, mate."

He could hear the lack of belief in his own voice. The throbbing pain that ran through Jake's hand seemed minor compared to Tom's injury and doing the only other thing he could think of, he removed his glasses and slid them over Tom's grey eyes.

Jake squinted as his face was pelted with debris and watched Tom turn to face him. Touching the glasses, Tom coughed and forced his words out. "I can't take these from you."

"It's the least I can do. It's my fault you're in this state. We'll get you sorted out, don't worry."

Fear ran through Jake's heart as he watched Tom's head fall to the side. How long would it be before he lost consciousness for good?

The sound of shifting rubble caught Jake's attention. Looking up, he saw that the distance between him and whatever was following them had been cut in half. It was a good job Tom was passed out; the last thing he needed was to be aware of that thing.

Jake got to his feet and picked up a brick. Letting its weight settle in his left hand, he yelled and lobbed it in the direction of the rubble.

The thing shifted back.

He grabbed another brick, threw it, and drove the thing back even farther.

"Now fuck off! I don't know what you want from us, but you ain't fucking getting it," he bellowed in rage.

Finding a glass bottle, he then shouted to the point where his throat felt like it was tearing and then hurled it with all this strength. The bottle was the best shot of all, scoring a direct hit on the rubble. The creature's hiss rose above the sound of shattering glass and Jake watched their stalker speed away from them. It travelled so quickly it was out of his view within seconds.

Remaining on his feet, he studied the horizon for signs of its return.

The sky had turned from gunmetal grey to black, making the hazy glow of the Rixon Tower even more prominent. Jake had kept a keen watch for the entire time and the thing hadn't returned. Maybe it was more scared of them than they were of it or maybe it had gone to get backup.

After hours of holding Tom's hand as he writhed in agony, Jake suddenly felt his friend's grip go limp. Watching the tall man roll over onto his side, Jake gasped when he stopped still and muttered, "Oh, fuck."

Just before Jake could check his pulse, Tom twitched. Although he could see his scarf moving, it was impossible to hear what Tom was saying. Jake leaned in close and listened to his weak voice whisper, "Can you get that for me please, Jake?"

Jake looked around but all he saw was rubbish. Raising a shaky hand, Tom pointed at a pile of rubble. Looking in the direction Tom was pointing Jake only saw bricks, old food wrappers, plastic bottles, and carrier bags. Turning back to his friend, he shrugged.

"What is it, Tom? What do you want?" He leaned close again to hear his reply.

"The ears."

Nestled in a crack in the ground between several large lumps of reinforced concrete was a black sphere made from toughened foam with two mouse ears. It was no bigger than a Ping-Pong ball and was the symbol of a corporate giant that, despite its prominence in the old world, was just a memory in the new one. The company that it represented was once so powerful they tried to buy Rixon. Jake was grateful they had failed; seeing the tower every day was sickening, but having two huge fucking ears on the horizon would have made him suicidal. When the attempted buyout failed, they did everything they could to compete with Rixon, but it was too late by then. Their technology was several years behind the German giant, so by the time the mouse had caught up, there were no consumers left. Everyone was hooked on New Reality.

Jake's muscles burned when he stood up. Stepping over Tom carefully, the wind threatening to knock his weak frame over, he made his way to the ears.

Once he'd picked them up, Jake held them in his left hand and examined them. It was strange that people had ever parted with their hard-earned money for such a useless item. The cost of it would have fed someone for a day in an impoverished nation. Jake's concave stomach rumbled at the thought of food.

Flipping the ears over, Jake looked at the hole in the bottom. It looked like it was designed to push a pen into. Shrugging, he walked back over to Tom and gave them to him.

The tall man's scarf lifted as if he were smiling beneath it. It was so much harder to read his expression now both his eyes and mouth were covered.

Several heavy coughs racked Tom's body. Groaning, he looked back at his trinket. "We used to have one of these …" he stopped to breathe, "…on the aerial of our car." Grief cracked his words. "Rory bought it."

"Of course," Jake said. "That's why I recognise them."

Oblivious to Jake's words, Tom dusted the ears off and continued smiling. A tear ran from beneath his glasses.

Jake leaned over again, placed his left hand on Tom's shoulder, and stared down at his friend.

After several breaths, Tom cleared his throat. "Rory …" Breaking down, he pulled the mouse ears into his chest.

Keeping his hand on Tom, Jake waited for him to speak again.

"He said he was going to use the headset…" He paused to breathe, "…to take him to Disney World. We'd never been." Several gulps later and Tom spoke with a weak voice. "He was desperate to go."

As Tom broke into another coughing fit, Jake could see he was tempering his hacking barks. The action was clearly jarring his hip.

"He was so excited, Jake." Shaking his head, Tom growled, "Then he put a fucking headset on."

Jake didn't reply.

"I knew it was a bad idea the second the straps closed around the back of his head… but it was too late by then."

"It was horrible to watch people put the headsets on," Jake agreed. His vision glazed as he relived the experience. "I remember the initial hit, or the 'set-up process' as Rixon called it, and how the users fell twitching to the floor. It was like watching people overdose on heroin. It's a wonder so many people still put a headset on after witnessing that."

Tom's voice broke when he said, "I shouldn't have let them put the headsets on at the same time, but they were so excited about the prospect and wanted to do it together. I lost them both; in one hit Rixon took everything from me."

"We'll find him, Tom, and we'll find a way to get the headset off."

When Tom lifted his glasses, Jake saw the light had left his eyes. "Like we did his mother you mean? Do I need to remind you we killed her? Every time I close my eyes, I see the image of her head bleeding into the rock."

"There must be a way to do it."

"If there is, we haven't found it. This is the end of the road for me, Jake." Resting his head against a slab of concrete, he stared up at the grey sky. "Besides, even if we do find him, what will happen? I'll roll him over to ease his pressure sores? Or rather," he paused to catch his breath, "I'll watch you roll him over. Or try to roll him over. He's probably huge by now and you only have one good hand. We're a pair of useless cripples, Jake."

Jake remained mute.

"We'll then spend days trying to work out a way to get his headset off." Snapping his body tight, Tom's face reddened as he groaned again. "We'll be lucky if we don't die of thirst while we're waiting, or get shot…" After a pause, he added, "Or get eaten by that horrible clickety-click thing."

Jake fought the urge to look behind him with the mention of the beasts. "We'll get the headset off, Tom."

"Let's say we do—" Letting out a sudden scream, Tom flipped onto his side and he lay there panting until he'd recovered.

"Then what? He'll be a slug and we'll have to spend the next few months, maybe years, running through physio with him. He won't be able to walk." Grunting again, his red face turned beetroot and he took shallow breaths. "None of his muscles will work, so we'll have to feed him and keep him hydrated. We can barely do that for ourselves."

Jake wished he had something to say.

"I realised months ago that it was too late for Rory." He coughed. "I've thought about it during every waking moment and I know there's *nothing* I can do for him. I don't know why I've kept going."

"Because some part of you believes—it must."

Shaking his head, Tom said, "No. I don't think that's it." The tall man then fell silent and his head lolled to the side.

After a minute or so had passed, Jake nudged him.

Tom continued as if he hadn't paused at all. "I think it's because I wanted to make amends for leaving him." Staring at the sky, he added, "Twice."

"You had to leave him. You had to find a way to take the headset off. They would have shot us if we'd gone back a second time."

"I should have been realistic. I should have just put a bloody headset on years ago." Reaching up, he grabbed Jake's left hand. "I'm done, Jake."

A wash of hot grief flushed Jake's face. "No, Tom."

Squeezing Jake's hand, Tom looked up. "Please just get me a headset."

With his bottom lip bending out of shape and heat stinging his eyeballs, Jake kept a hold of his friend's hand but looked away.

"I can't even walk, Jake."

Jake turned back to Tom. Staring at his broken form for a short time, he then dropped a gentle nod. "Okay."

***

She clasped her hands before her and said in a low murmur, "Good boy, Jake."

With a grin stretching wide on her face, she sat back and watched Jake get to his feet. Finally! They were going to separate.

Chapter Twenty-Nine

Other than the occasional groan and whimper, Tom had been virtually inanimate all night. The slight rise and fall of Tom's chest was the only sign he was still alive.

"It's morning now, mate," Jake said. "Sorry I haven't left sooner, but you know what it's like traveling at night. I'll find you a headset, pal, just hang on in there."

Jake's arms shook as grabbed the cold pylon with his left hand and pulled himself to his feet. The effort increased his heart rate and the throb in his palm reminded him of his infection.

Keeping a hold of the metal structure, Jake adjusted to the onslaught of the wind while the deafening gales wrapped his head in blusterous chaos. Turning around, he searched behind. There was still no sign of the thing following them. Where had it gone?

Jake looked down at Tom and sighed. "See you later, mate."

He ducked through a gap in the metal skeleton, every muscle in his malnourished body screaming in burning protest. Straightening his back once he was through the other side, Jake groaned as a series of clicks ran down his spine. He rolled his shoulders and tried to block out the pain in his hand. The angry throb sent shards of electric pain into his wrist. Shaking the thought from his mind, he looked one last time for the line of rubble that had been following them. So far, so good—there was nothing there.

Facing the fierce wind, he dipped his head into it and began his wobbly ascent out of the valley.

With nothing to pull himself up by and what little energy he had draining from his legs, it took Jake about fifteen minutes to shuffle halfway up the hill. A mixture of grit and perspiration stung his eyes. Wiping his brow, he searched the valley floor for signs of raised rubble— nothing. Jake shook his head. It would have been foolish to believe the thing had gone.

"Just bloody show yourself," he growled into his scarf.

He thought of Tom writhing in pain where he had left him and a frown darkened Jake's face. How far would he have to walk to find a headset? What if he didn't find one at all? There would come a point where turning back wouldn't make sense. How long would it be before he wrote his best friend off? What if the thing…

Something moving under the ground caught Jake's eye. It raced towards Tom, kicking up bricks and stones as it sped across the wasteland.

"Oh, no. Fuck, no!" Jake choked out.

With his pulse racing, Jake searched his surroundings for something that could help Tom. There was nothing useful. When he looked back up, he saw the thing wasn't stopping.

"Tom!" he cried. His word was carried away on the strong wind like an empty crisp packet.

"Tom!" he screamed.

He quickly bent down and picked up a rock; maybe the clanging metal would alert his friend. Putting everything he had into it, he yelled as he lobbed the rock at the pylon. It fell woefully short.

"Tom!" The wind was so loud he could barely hear himself. How could he expect Tom to hear him?

Just as Jake was about to run down the hill, he lost sight of the thing. Frowning, he scanned the valley. Where had it gone?

Then he saw the ground move again. It had stopped about fifteen metres away from his friend. What was it doing?

The wind rocked Jake as he stood on the hill and watched the immobile lump of raised rubble. Having spent at least half an hour waiting, the thing hadn't moved. He couldn't wait there all day. It wasn't just the thing beneath the ground that was Tom's enemy. Time was sharpening its scythe too. The mission hadn't changed. The only thing Jake could do was find a headset.

Taking a few steps up the hill, Jake turned around again. The thing still hadn't moved; a few more steps and a check, nothing. A few more steps…

Once he was at the top of the hill, Jake scanned what he could see of the wasteland stretching before him. One more step forwards and he'd have to forget about his friend until he found a headset. Jake was now too far away to see what the thing was doing and could barely see Tom anymore. Watching the blurred image of his companion, he gulped and—although he wasn't sure why—he said, "God be with you, Tom." As he turned back around, he caught a flash of movement in his peripheral vision. He tried to trace the streak of black as it vanished into the grainy air but quickly gave up and looked at what it had left behind.

Lying just metres away from him were two shiny black headsets. The scarlet stripes of their corporate branding ran across them. Looking again for what must have been the Bot that dropped them off; all Jake saw was dust clouds and devastation.

Jake shook his head and looked at the offering, his body tense. He then looked up at the glowing tower on the horizon. Tom was right, they *were* watching them.

"Fuck you, Rixon. This is all just a fucking game to you, isn't it?" he yelled out in anger and frustration.

There was no reply. Why would there be? Staring at what he could see of the tower, Jake let his hand fall to his side; it was just a tower. The god inside the machine was faceless and omnipotent. It acted when it was inclined to do so, not because it was goaded by an insignificant ant.

Jake had to hurry up. His choice was clear—one headset or two?

Holding his grumbling stomach, he looked at the small white tube in each. Sustenance stared back at him. In one of those black plastic shells was a potential escape from his hellish existence. All he'd seen in a long while was ruin and decay. Nature had abandoned this world a long time ago. Why was he still searching for it?

He rubbed his face, stepped forwards, and groaned as he leaned over. Using his functioning left hand, Jake lifted the headsets; their combined weight was heavy on his weak arm. How much of their burden was physical, and how much was psychological? Jake was just about to do the one thing he swore he'd never do. Just the action of holding them was like signing a deal with the devil.

The headsets swayed in the breeze like coconuts and the throbbing in Jake's hand increased. It was like his body was spurring him on. The infection seemed to be getting worse by the second.

Two days away from dehydration, a week from starvation, and a thing at his back that was thirsty for his blood left him just one choice. Jake's frame sagged. Tom was right; this was as good as it got.

***

Take your time, Jake. Take as much time as you like. Don't worry about Tom. I have my eye on him. The tension in her shoulders eased as she let out a relieved sigh. *He'll probably be dead before you get back anyway...*

Chapter Thirty

Jake was about to return to Tom when he saw a dark blur vanish behind a pile of broken plasterboard. Staring for a moment, Jake's blood suddenly ran cold and he tried not to panic. Why hadn't he seen it before it happened? These bloody headsets weren't a gift. They were a trap.

Loosening his grip on the straps, Jake was about to let the headsets fall, but he stopped. That was a ridiculous idea. What would he do, pretend he'd never seen them and deny any wrongdoing? Like that would prevent him from receiving a belly full of lead.

The machine had been sent with a mission. It had executed it flawlessly. Shaking his head, Jake's body trembled. What a mug! Why had he fallen for it?

He pulled his shoulders back and shouted at the pile of broken plasterboard, "Come on then, you piece of shit! I'm here if you want me!"

He was about to open his mouth to shout again, when he saw another movement. Falling into a defensive crouch, he let the headsets hang from his hand like a slingshot.

When he saw movement again, he relaxed a little. It wasn't a Bot behind the broken boards; it was a flap of material blowing in the gales. Laughing, he straightened his back.

Both the throb in his right arm and good sense told him to take the headsets back to his friend. Despite this, he took a couple of steps in the direction of the fabric. The shifting surface was a terrible platform should he need to beat a hasty retreat, but he had to see what was there.

Arriving at the boards, he peered over. The first thing to hit him was the putrefying and rancid smell. Although he pinched his nose, he was too slow and was left with the taste of decay in his mouth.

After just a few seconds, his infected hand burned and made pinching his nose too hard to bear. Letting go, he continued to hold the headsets with his other hand and tried to breathe through his mouth as he studied the form before him.

The billowing material was a sweatshirt. All that was left of it clung to the gamer's right wrist and rode the elements like a tattered flag. The rest of the gamer's body was exposed. The huge torso had clearly burst free of its clothes years before. The bulbous chin of the gamer moved with his phlegmy irregular breaths. It was like listening to someone with sleep apnea.

Jake looked at the long ginger hair and scarred top lip. The remaining fabric bore the logo of Aston Villa Football Club. Running his left hand through his greasy hair, Jake sighed. "Oh, fuck."

***

Her sore eyes widened and her breath caught in her throat. *Shit!* This could ruin everything. Tom needed to be gone for Jake to survive. If he found out about his son, he wouldn't put the headset on. That would stop Jake from moving on. If he didn't leave Birmingham, she'd have to get involved.

Balling her right hand into a fist, she bit down on it. *Shit!*

Chapter Thirty-One

When Jake looked down the hill, his breath left his lungs. Tom was gone. Opening his mouth to call out, Jake stopped. What good would it do? It was impossible to be heard over the wind.

Jake ground his jaw as he frowned against the elements and thought. Had the creature got to Tom? He looked for a tell-tale line leading up to where Tom was, but saw nothing.

Jake rode the hill of loose debris as cautiously as he could with his weak legs threatening to give out beneath him. Arriving at the pylon without falling, he bobbed and weaved through the metal structure, pausing twice to catch his breath.

When Jake came out of the other side of the metal structure, he saw his friend lying exactly where he'd left him. He now lay totally flat and hidden by the pylon, which must have been why Jake thought he was gone. Blinking against the sting of sweat running into his eyes, Jake sighed. "Thank fuck."

The relief passed quickly. The tall man appeared to be sleeping, but Jake had expected some sort of reaction from him. "Tom?"

There was no movement from the man.

"Tom?"

Still nothing.

Dropping a little too quickly, Jake's kneecaps cracked against a particularly robust slab of concrete. The shock ran up his body and made him drop the headset. He tried to ignore the pain as he leaned over and touched Tom's cold face.

"Tom, are you okay, mate?" he said as he pulled the sunglasses away—Tom's eyes were closed.

When he still didn't move, Jake slid two fingers along his neck. It was hard to tell for certain through the dusty beard, but he couldn't feel a pulse.

"Tom, wake up." Jake shook him gently but there was still no response.

Running his hand through his hair, Jake looked at the headset. He'd brought it to him too late. Grief twisted both his face and voice. "Come on, man, wake up. I went as quickly as I could."

Jake closed his eyes and faced the sky. "Please, God, let him be okay. I have a headset for him now. Please."

"What are you doing?" Tom asked in a feeble voice.

It jolted Jake from his prayer, and he looked down at his friend. "You bastard, I thought you'd died. Jesus, man, don't do that to me."

When Tom regarded Jake, it was clear death wasn't far away.

Grabbing the headset, Jake offered it to him. "Here, I managed to find one."

Tom shook his head. "How?"

"It was just over the brow of the hill."

Jake could see Tom grinning beneath his scarf. "What are you so happy about?"

"They heard us. After all these years…" Pausing, Tom closed his eyes, and took several breaths, "…of being watched. It's finally paid off."

The image of the naked and obese Rory filled Jake's mind. Someone had been watching him when he was with Tom's son. What did they think he should do now? Should he tell him? Would they think he was a bad person if he withheld the information? Would they punish him for it? At a loss for words, he handed the headset over and remained silent.

Tom dipped a weak nod at his friend. "Thank you. I know you don't agree with me putting this on, but I feel like it's what I need to do for the sake of my sanity."

The scarred top lip. The long ginger hair. The stretch marks. When he realised Tom was awaiting a response, Jake shook his head and tried to focus. "Um, so what will you do in New Reality?"

"I'll eat and drink with my family."

Jake's empty stomach gurgled, and his dry throat ached. "That sounds nice."

Looking at the mouse ears, Tom laughed before spiralling into hacking coughs. When he finished, he looked paler than ever, but he was still smiling. "I think we'll go to Disney World."

It pleased Jake to see his friend happy. It was the first time in what felt like years. He thought of Rory and forced a smile of his own. What would it do to Tom to see his son as the grotesque slug he'd just left behind?

"What's wrong, Jake?"

Snapping out of his daydream, the grin still sitting awkwardly on his face, Jake looked at his friend. "Huh?" His mind quickly caught up and he added, "Nothing. Why?"

What appeared to be another hot wave of pain ran through the grimacing Tom. Once it had passed, he said, "You look a little," his eyes rolled, his last word coming out in a delirious sigh, "preoccupied."

"I'm fine. It's just…" Jake stared at the headset. "I'm sad you're going, man."

The look in Tom's eyes showed he knew there was more.

Looking away, Jake said, "And there was something else over the brow of the hill."

When Tom reached across and grabbed Jake's hand, Jake flinched. "You're cold, Tom."

"Don't change the subject. What else did you see over the brow of the hill?"

Angry red stretch marks. The Aston Villa Football Club logo.

"There were two headsets." His cheeks flushed with his half-lie.

"So why didn't you take one for yourself?"

Shrugging, Jake looked at the Rixon Tower. It was easier than looking at his friend. "I know nature will win out. I want to see it happen."

In the past, Jake's comment would have been met with resistance; this time though, Tom squeezed Jake's hand again and nodded. "I hope it does. You deserve to see your dream fulfilled."

Tom's sincerity was a knife to Jake's stomach. The last few years of Tom's life had been about finding his son and Jake now held the power to make that happen.

"Come on, just put the bloody thing on and be done with it. Let's not drag this out and get all sentimental, eh?" Looking away, Jake blinked to clear the tears from his eyes.

Tom lifted the headset over his head. The device cast a thick shadow over Tom's long face.

Raising his hand, Jake said, "Wait."

Tom paused.

"Good luck, man. Sweet dreams and all that. I really hope it works out for you and you get everything you wish for."

Tom smiled. "I will." He then said, "Jake."

Avoiding eye contact, Jake watched the hazy sun. "Yeah?"

"You've never told me about your life before New Reality. You've only ever talked about the future."

Shrugging, Jake still didn't look down at his friend. "There's nothing to talk about."

"I'd like to hear it anyway."

Jake picked up a rock and stared at it as he spoke, "I had two parents that fully supported everything I did. For a while, I was an only child." Pausing, he cleared the hot lump of grief wedged in his throat. "Well, I ended up an only child."

"Ended up?"

Jake tried to clear his throat again. "Louisa died when she was five. Leukaemia. I was eight at the time." Staring into the distance, he continued, "The hospital was such a positive place. It was full of bald children who all knew they'd get better."

After a sigh, he looked down at Tom. "Louisa was one of the few that didn't. Positivity didn't help her much and chemo stuck the boot in. She got progressively worse."

When Tom's grey eyes pinched, Jake laughed. "I bet you regret asking now, eh?"

Shaking his head, Tom said in a weak voice, "Not at all. The children's ward was the worst in the entire hospital when I was working there... so bright and colourful; so many deaths. What about your parents? How did they cope?"

"Badly. They went to pieces. We all did. Once the death of a child enters your house, it never leaves. Mum did her best but Dad was distant after that. He didn't want to play football in the park anymore. He didn't want to go on family outings. He didn't want to leave his armchair.

The TV was always on and Dad was always staring at it. He also drank a lot more. He was never a horrible drunk, just distant."

When Tom winced in sympathy at his friend, Jake pointed at him. "Don't you fucking dare!"

Tom frowned.

"That face. That face that says 'I know how you feel' or 'I'm sorry'. Don't, Tom, not you."

Tom raised his eyebrows and nodded before saying, "So what about your parents? Did they put headsets on?"

"No. But if Dad had still been alive when New Reality came out, he'd have been first in the queue. He wouldn't have been able to resist the opportunity to get lost in the ultimate coping mechanism."

Shaking his head, Jake drew a deep and stuttered breath. "We had a lovely little house with a balcony that faced the road. Dad covered that balcony with teddies. He thought his shrine looked like something from a fairy tale. It didn't. It was fucking weird. It looked like something from a horror movie. It was mental. He'd buy new teddies for each season—Easter bunnies, bears dressed as Santa, stuffed witches. We had hundreds of them stored in Louisa's old room. It was like he was expecting her to come back. Passers-by would ask what they were for and we'd say it was a charity thing. People didn't need our sadness."

When Jake looked over to see Tom staring at him, he bit his bottom lip and his eyes burned with tears. "Mum died of cancer too. After that, Dad just stopped..."

Pausing, he searched his mind for an appropriate word. "...working." He tested the phrase. "He just stopped working. His batteries ran out. When I visited him, he'd just stare out of the window into the garden. The loud tick of his clock and the chink of the ice in his whisky glass were about the only sounds in his house from then on. When he died, he left everything to me. My parents had a lot of money, so I never had to work again." Looking at the red glow on the horizon, Jake sneered. "I had a life of lazy luxury mapped out before Rixon fucked it all up."

When he looked down at Tom, he was surprised to see him crying. The wind wobbled the tears on his face. "You've been a good friend, Jake."

The words twisted Jake's stomach.

"I'll miss you."

Jake's throat tightened and his vision glazed. Clearing his throat again, he chewed the inside of his mouth.

"If you see Rory out there, tell him I love him." Grabbing Jake's good hand, Tom's eyes held a sharp focus. "Tell him I tried."

Unable to speak, Jake nodded and tears rolled down his cheeks.

"Thank you, Jake, you're a good man. Your parents would be proud of you."

Jake shook uncontrollably and looked away—if only he knew.

Pulling his scarf away from his mouth, Tom said, "I love you, Jake. I'm sorry I'm leaving." He lifted the headset and then paused.

"And Jake."

Jake looked up.

"Be careful of whatever's been following us. They're malicious creatures. I saw nothing but hate in their dark eyes."

Jake could only nod and watch as Tom placed the headset over his head.

The headset's black straps came to life and wrapped around the back of Tom's head like a spider entrapping its prey. Several twitches pulsed through Tom's long frame before he fell limp like every muscle had failed simultaneously.

Jake stared at his friend. Tom's body had yielded to the uneven terrain. Joining the rest of the inanimate idiots, Tom was now no more than a corpse with a pulse.

"I'm sorry, Tom. I truly am." Suddenly Tom's chest jumped towards the sky as his back arched. Staring at him, Jake frowned. "Tom?"

The man's body fell limp again and Jake continued to watch. Then his headset fell away. The light had left Tom's grey eyes and his face was slack.

"Tom?" Jake said as he gingerly shook him.

When Jake saw a line of blood leaking from the corner of Tom's mouth, he got to his feet and tried to sit him up. At first, he was hard to move, but then he came free and flipped over onto his front. Jake's legs weakened as he looked down at the metal spike then to the blood covering it, and finally to the hole in Tom's back.

Suddenly the ground came to life and something shot away from them, spraying Jake with stones and masonry. Within seconds it was out of view.

Jake stared at the bloody spike and shook as rage filled his senses. He looked into the distance where the thing had disappeared and then looked back down at the spike again. Clenching his fists and gritting his teeth against the burn in his right hand, he screamed until his throat was raw.

Jake dropped to his knees, and with tears streaming from his sore eyes, he stared at his dead friend.

***

With her hand on her pounding heart, she pulled deep breaths into her tight lungs. It was like she'd been stabbed herself. There was no doubt that Tom had to go. It was important that she reminded herself that. Tom had to go. To keep him alive would be to keep Jake in Birmingham. Her orders were clear. If Jake didn't move on, she had to end him. If her superiors found how long she'd let Jake live already, there'd be consequences.

She glanced from Tom's dead body to look at his grieving friend. If Tom had drifted off into New Reality, there'd always be a reason for Jake to come back and check on him. Although it didn't make it any easier, it had to end this way for Tom. He was a good friend to Jake, but he was in the way.

Looking at Jake's hunched form, she felt every one of his tears. Watching the skinny and broken man, she drew a deep sigh and spoke under her breath. "He's gone now, Jake. You need to move on for your own sake. You need to get out of the city. If you don't, you'll die."

Chapter Thirty-Two

Sitting still for so long had left a stagnant burn in Jake's joints. He flinched in anticipation of the pain as he stretched out and when he straightened his legs, he felt like his kneecaps would crack. He frowned hard and pushed through the sensations.

It was only when he touched his sodden cheeks that he realised he was still crying.

Looking at the corpse of his friend, who was still on his side, the back of his shirt damp with blood, Jake heaved a deep sigh and the tears surged again. Maybe Tom was with Thalia now.

"I'm sorry we didn't save her, man. I should never have rushed you, but a Bot was bearing down on her.

"I should have told you about Rory too. Although I didn't think it would help. What could you have done with your hip like it is?"

Jake laughed. "It's a wonder we lasted as long as we did though." The scar in his arm ached. "After having my wing clipped by a Rixon-Bot, I thought I was done for. How did we survive for so long, Tom?"

###

The effort of climbing out of the crater for a second time was almost too much for Jake's body. When he arrived at the top of the hill, panting, he heaved several times. The exertion had also irritated his infected hand, the burn now crawling round his back as it clung to his shoulder blade with a rusty grip.

As everything levelled out and the pain receded, Jake looked down at his friend one the last time. His best friend. The man deserved a eulogy, but Jake didn't have the words.

Jake stared for a moment longer then dropped his eyes to a broken headstone that lay by his feet. The image brought everything flooding back. The night on the tombstone, the creatures beneath it, scratching... the inscription.

Jake opened his mouth to speak but was too choked. Drawing several breaths, he finally said, "Happy birthday, mate."

Jake gave a quick nod, dropped his shoulders, and turned his back on him forever.

***

As she watched Jake walk away with his body slumped and feet dragging, she tried to ignore the feeling of her brothers and sisters around her. It was against the rules to even look at one another, but that didn't mean someone wasn't doing it. Did they know she'd let Jake live for as long as she had? If there was a checklist for termination, Jake would have ticked every box several times already. She should have ended him by now.

Holding her hands as if in prayer; she tapped the tips of her fingers together and watched him walk away. If she could protect him until he got out of the city, then no one would need to know that she should have terminated him. There was hope for Jake yet. He just needed to hurry the hell up.

Chapter Thirty-Three

The wind continued to flick the strip of material on Rory's wrist and his Aston Villa logo was still on display. Even if he wasn't aware of it, the boy still waved his colours with pride. Jake sighed—a shared love between father and son of a football team; memories of weekends in the stadium; the highs, the lows, the bonding. The claret and blue team colours now faded to almost grey along with the memories Rory would have had with Tom.

Both of Jake's knees popped like snapping twigs when he squatted down next to Rory. The sensation was nothing unusual and he wondered how long would it be before his damaged body refused to get back up again.

Drawing a deep breath, Jake pushed into the top of Rory's right arm with his left hand. The fat on the kid's bicep squeezed through Jake's fingers, but Rory didn't budge.

After a short rest, Jake clenched his teeth and pushed again. Even though his arm was shaking, his damaged right hand throbbed, and his eyeballs felt like they would pop, he kept pushing until stars swam in his vision. When his head started to spin, Jake yielded and fell back onto his arse as he panted from the effort.

Once he'd recovered, Jake stared at the boy. "I'm sorry, Rory, I can't flip you over. If Tom were here, then we'd be able to do it, but..." He looked down at the bloody bandage on his right hand and his starved body. "I struggle to lift my own weight now."

Exhaustion ran through his veins like tar. Hunger ate him away from the inside. His saliva had turned into a thick and dusty paste in his throat.

The second headset was exactly where he'd left it, lying next to Rory and rocking in the wind. For an item that had caused more devastation to the human race than any other invention before it, it seemed so innocuous. It had spread throughout the world without prejudice like a virus. What was Rixon's end goal? What would they do when everyone was dead? How do you manipulate a society with no people? Looking up at the glow on the horizon, he shook his head and lifted his lip in a sneer. Tom was right; there were people left in the tower. There had to be.

But what good would it do to think about that now?

After studying Rory's obese form, Jake closed his eyes and took a deep breath. "I didn't tell your dad about you, Rory. I'm sorry, but with his hip and my hand, there was no way of getting him to you. I figured that if he didn't know you were here, then he could move on without guilt. If I'd told him, he'd have refused to put the headset on and died dragging himself to you. I didn't want that to happen."

Rory's huge chin wobbled and he grunted as he fought for breath. Snorting an ironic laugh, Jake shook his head.

Once he'd levelled out and fallen back into his pattern of laboured respiration, Jake continued, "I didn't want his last thoughts to be tormented by the fact that you were so close but totally unreachable.

"Besides, even if we *had* managed to get to you, we couldn't get that bloody thing off your head anyway." Leaning forward and touching his cold arm, Jake spoke slower. "I hope you understand."

With tears blurring his vision, Jake's voice cracked. "He said he was going to have dinner with you and your mum in Disney World. That was his plan anyway.

"Whatever's been following us killed him, Rory." Jake glanced over his shoulder then looked back down at the boy. "I swear to you, if it's the last thing I do, I'll avenge your father's death."

The pain of standing up tore through Jake and fresh tears slid down his face. Watching Rory's heavy chest rise and fall, Jake allowed the grief to flow out of him.

When he was done, he swallowed the burning lump in his throat. "Your dad was a good man. He's the reason I'm still alive. In those early days, when I felt like I couldn't go on, I looked at him and his unwavering determination to get to you. His purpose became my purpose and it gave me hope—a reason to carry on. His determination to get to you was so fierce it took a broken hip to stop him.

"He saved my life too. It was nuts. I thought I was done for but your dad saved me. I owe him my life, Rory. I didn't know him before all of this bullshit happened, but I can honestly…" Grief choked him. "I can honestly say he's the best friend I've ever had."

After rocking in the wind for a few seconds, he turned his attention back to Rory. "I also wanted to thank you. Seeing you here has made me realise that I *will* find what I'm looking for. Your dad wanted to give up, and you were waiting around the next corner. It's taught me never to do the same." Crouching down, he patted the boy's fat arm. Ripples rolled away from the point of impact. "Sweet dreams, son. Take care."

He stood up again, turned his back on Rory, dipped his head against the oncoming wind, and strode off with more purpose than he'd felt in a long time. Nature would win out. Things would change.

***

She leaned back and let the tension of the last few weeks run out of her shoulders. This was it, the start of Jake's new life without Tom. It wouldn't be long and he'd be out of Birmingham. The city was the last thing Jake needed to be free of before he could move on and she could stop watching him.

As Jake walked, she could see the determination in his stride. Sure, he'd lost his best friend, but his purpose had been revitalised. Everything was going to work out.

Throwing glances over each shoulder at those surrounding her, she saw no one was watching. She was going to get away with not killing him.

Chapter Thirty-Four

Seeing Rory had given Jake hope. What he was searching for was out there. All he could do about Tom now was learn from him. While gritting his teeth, he let his new mantra spin through his mind and pace his steps. *Never give up. Never give up. Never give up. Never give up.*

The mental pep talk helped Jake move with greater ease. The infection that had a hold of his right arm was receding. His joints moved with fluidity. A little too confident in his miraculous healing, he clenched his right fist. The burn made his stomach lurch and his head spin. *Maybe that was a step too far,* he thought.

Jake squared his shoulders and lifted his face into the stormy winds. *Never give up. Never give up.*

Stopping just before he slipped on it, Jake looked down at the bottle of water in front of him. It looked exactly the same as the one Tom had found—almost as if it had come from the same place. Jake looked around and couldn't see anything unusual but for all he knew, he was surrounded by Bots on all sides. Cameras could be feeding back to the tower right now, showing his every action.

"Fuck it," he said into the wind. Bending down, he lifted the bottle and flipped the lid off with his left hand. The movement ran an arthritic burn through his joints and his fingers were too stiff to stop the cap from floating away on the wind. He shook his head as he watched it fly away and then lifted the plastic bottle to his lips to let the cool liquid fill his dry mouth.

Upending the bottle and draining it of its last bit of water, Jake let the container go. The liquid swilled in his stomach and he would have liked to save some for later but without a lid the water would be contaminated with grit by the time he tried to drink it.

Clearing his throat of the burn nestling at the back of it, Jake lifted the scarf covering his mouth, spat, and set off again.

That was when he saw it.

At first, hidden by the dust storm, it looked like another mound of debris. But as he got closer, he saw its form had more order than that.

Halving the distance between him and the mound, he stopped. It was a church spire. The building was clearly buried far below it. The slightest smile lifted the sides of his mouth. Looking up at the sky, he laughed. "Not even Rixon can topple the big man."

Jake walked closer and looked up at the top of it. What was protruding from the rubble stood only about ten feet high—he was a long way from what used to be ground level.

The old tiles that clung to the structure looked like they should have been replaced years previously, but despite the harsh elements, they still clung on.

Walking around the other side, Jake found a hole big enough to poke his head into and see if there was maybe a way down. He wondered if there was food and water in the unintentional catacombs; the world below must be ripe for mining. If only he could get to it.

Staring at the craggy mouth, its dark throat a deep well, Jake looked at the snapped wooden batons stretching across the space. The roof looked like a ribcage with a hole blown through it.

As the strong wind raced down the hole like water finding the path of least resistance, Jake listened to the church push it back out again. The strong gales were returned with a gentle sigh.

A chill ran through Jake and his toes curled. The building sounded like it was alive. Shaking his head, he forced a laugh and spoke for what he quickly realised was the benefit of the building. "It's just the wind, stop being such a pussy."

Jake stepped closer and listened. Inhale, sigh, inhale, sigh. Standing on tiptoes, he peered in and found utter and complete darkness.

Despite every part of Jake's being telling him to walk away, he edged farther forwards. Inhale, sigh, inhale, sigh.

When Jake was just a step away, he smelled the church's dusty breath. The stale air reeked of rot like mouldy wood; or old bones.

Jake took a deep breath and poked his head through the gap. The stench was worse inside and it forced him to screw his nose up. Although Jake couldn't see it, he could feel the emptiness stretching out below him—the place was huge. How would he get down there?

Then he heard a scratching sound…

The thing!

It was still following him.

"No. Not again," Jake whispered as he shook his head.

Grinding his teeth, he pushed his face farther into the hole and screamed into the empty space. "Fuck off, you piece of shit!"

The call flew through the building. It found every corner of the cavernous space and returned an ever-diminishing, "SHIT, SHit, shit," back to him.

The scratching stopped.

Holding his breath, Jake listened.

Silence.

Just as he was about to turn and walk away, he heard something. It was a guttural and mewling growl that was somewhere between a cry and a cough.

"*Shit*."

It was mimicking him.

A shadow moved through the darkness far below. It was as if the object was a deeper shade of black than the pitch of the church—like it was on a different light spectrum.

The sound of Jake's panicked breath bounced back at him as he scanned the emptiness and shouted, "Just fucking show yourself."

The shadow moved again. It moved fast and made the clickety-click scuttling noise he'd heard when they were being chased by an army of them. It stopped where Jake could see it; or at least see a darker blob of black. Its voice was clearer but still deep and rattling like a phlegmy cough. It repeated the word like it had no understanding of its meaning. "Shit."

Jake bent down and lifted a rock from near his feet. When he looked back in, the blob was still there. Putting all of his effort into it, Jake grunted as he launched the rock.

It crashed against what sounded like a stone floor below and the creature responded with a scorpion's hiss.

Pulling his head from the hole, Jake backed away. He picked up another rock and lobbed it from where he was standing. The hissing grew louder.

Backing away some more, he threw another. It missed but dislodged three tiles that all fell into the void. Three distant smashes were followed by a growl that made the thing sound closer than ever.

Forgetting his aches and injuries, Jake turned and was about to run until he heard something that froze him in his tracks.

"Jake Weston."

How did it know his name? Jake broke into a run despite his brittle legs aching as if the bones would crumble beneath him.

"Jake Weston. Jake Weston." The voice remained the same volume despite the distance he was putting between them. It was a dark and unique accent like the creature came from a secluded corner of a distant rainforest and was speaking English for the first time. It nestled in his memories next to the bloody eyes and started to complete the picture of the monster. It was more cunning, more brutal, and more ruthless than he could ever be. It was also clearly comfortable on a terrain that bipeds weren't ever meant to thrive on. To fight it was foolish.

As he looked back over his shoulder while he ran away, the surface suddenly gave way beneath Jake and he fell. Landing across a bar on his way down, his back made a tearing crack like splintering wood and he was enveloped by a fireball of agony.

The fall was luckily only about six feet and as Jake lay on his back, staring up at the hole he'd made while debris fell in on him, he groaned.

Then his world went dark.

***

Balling her right fist, she punched her left hand. *Fuck! All he had to do was leave Birmingham.* After that, she was sure he'd have seen the potential for a positive existence.

But no, not Jake Weston. Too bloody curious that man. Didn't he know it wasn't nice to throw rocks?

As she watched him, as he lay on his back out cold, she shook her head. *I'm sorry, Jake, but this has to end now.*

Chapter Thirty-Five

Opening his eyes, Jake saw dust swirling in the air above him as if he'd only just fallen. Maybe he had. It was hard to tell.

Bang! The sound was like a horse kicking a stable door.

Adrenaline surged through Jake but his limbs were lead and his back ached. Riding the rush, he took quick breaths and stared up at hole he'd fallen through. The wind above raged as fiercely as before, but inside there was a musty stillness. It was like he'd fallen into a tomb—perhaps his own.

Bang!

"Fuck." Lifting his head, Jake pulled air through his clenched teeth. It felt like his vertebrae were being separated with hot knives. *Broken back?* He wiggled his toes. *No.*

Bang!

Taking huge gulps of the musty air, Jake sat up, wincing with every millimetre of movement. He was on a bus. What the hell? It was a double-decker and he was riding on the top deck. The top always afforded the best view of the city; although all he saw through this bus's windows was rubble. Were it not for the hole he'd created, then it would be pitch black inside.

Bang! Bang!

The bus shook and Jake grabbed on, his damaged right hand screaming from the movement. Finding a rock on the floor, Jake picked it up and got to his feet.

Bang!

The sound was coming from the rear of the bus. Hunched over, Jake stared in the direction of the noise.

Bang!

This had to end now. Stepping forwards and straightening his back, Jake nearly vomited before he got his words out. "Show yourself, you coward."

Bang! Bang! Bang!

A thick cloud of dust rose into the air and Jake stopped still. Looking at the rock in his hand, he dropped it on the wooden floor. *Who am I kidding? There was no way I can stand toe to toe with it,* he told himself.

Bang!

The entire bus shook again and Jake thrust his arms out for balance.

Bang!

Jake kept his eyes on the back corner of the bus and took a step back. When he bumped into one of the old seats, it rocked on its rusty hinges. If the inside was ruined, what was the outside of the bus like? How long would it be before the thing burst through the rusty shell?

There was a scrabbling sound and the debris along the bottom of the large back window shifted.

The dust in the air got into Jake's throat and it itched when he swallowed a sandy gulp. Jake looked up. He was directly beneath the hole he'd fallen through.

More ruins shifted on the other side of the back window and when Jake saw a hand, he froze. "What the...?"

It looked human, but where the fingernails should have been there were black crusts of dried blood. A life underground seemed to have no need of them.

Jake looked up but the hole above seemed impossibly out of reach.

After pulling some more stones away, an arm rubbed along the back window. Its movements were frantic as it fought the environment to get to its prey. The pallid appendage had dark veins running along it as if it had oil for blood. The creature hissed.

Jake lifted one of his legs, gritted his teeth against the pain of his spine feeling like it was about to click out of place and when he'd raised it high enough to get onto the seat, he stepped up

Using his left hand, Jake grabbed the handrail above although a wobble shook his entire body. He stretched a leg across and straddled the aisle to place a foot on the back of each chair. The seats rocked beneath him and sent ripples up his spine that made the muscles in his back spasm. If he didn't hurry up, the seats would tear free of their bolts and throw him back down to where he'd come from.

Long dark hair framing a pale forehead appeared at the window. It was a little girl! Squirming, she slithered up the rubble and cleared a path with her head.

Taking several deep breaths, Jake shook his head in astonishment when he saw the little girl's face. She was no more than eight years old. The grease in her hair made it thick. Nestled in sunken sockets were the bloody eyes he'd seen in the house. A glazing of deep red sat where irises and retinas should have been.

Three, two, one. Jake pushed for the hole.

Rising out of it, he brought his elbows crashing down on the outside of the bus, but there was nothing to latch onto. Slipping, he kicked his legs, fell backwards into the hole, and hit the ground with a thud.

His body writhed and contorted on the floor as Jake choked on the dusty air. When he looked up at the window, he saw the girl lying diagonally across it like a lizard on a hot tile. Her bloody eyes locked at him, she hissed, banged on the window and snapped her jaws.

The hiss rang in Jake's ears as he sat up again, his abused body slow to cooperate. He got back up, lifted his leg, and stood up on the seats again. The rusty bolts groaned under his weight for a second time.

She banged it against the window with a clenched fist; determined to reach him.

Jake stretched his damaged arm to the sky and reached for the lip of the hole. Some of the rust at the edges crumpled like ash but he found a piece that he thought would support his weight and grabbed it.

Bang!

Raising his left hand, he found a place to grab opposite his right. With sweat running into his eyes, he glanced back at the girl. Hatred twisted her evil features.

Bang! A crack appeared on the back window.

Jake's right foot slipped off the seat. Clinging onto the lip of the hole with his left hand, he prevented a fall but his back crackled as his body jarred.

Bang! The window creaked as the crack stretched.

Looking down at his dangling feet, Jake found the backs of the seats again.

Bang!

Just as he got his footing, the window popped with a *whoosh!* A solid thud as she hit the floor followed and was accompanied by tingling glass and crashing rubble.

Jake bent his knees, his strength having all but vanished from his legs, and looked up out of the hole.

One last glance into the bus showed the girl spring up and land in a crouch. Hissing again, she ran at him, her bare feet pattering against the wooden floor.

Jake took a deep breath, pushed off, and jumped for daylight.

Jake found a lump of metal and grabbed it with his left hand when he poked out of the hole. As he pulled himself up, the girl hit his dangling foot, but Jake managed to get free before she could pull him back in.

Scrambling away, Jake fell onto his side and gasped. With blurred vision, he stared at the devastation surrounding him and his body felt like it would never work again.

Jake listened as he lay there; despite the strong wind, he could hear the snarling and hissing in the bus below.

Once Jake had recovered, he got to his feet. The dirt on the wind stuck to his sweaty face and he shook violently. He walked over to the hole on wobbly legs and peered in.

She kept her face turned towards Jake while pacing up and down the aisle. Her red eyes glared death and her open mouth was a black pit.

Jake stared at the creature below. Despite having a human form, her actions were alien. There was a twitchiness to her gait that Jake had never seen in a living creature. "What are you going to do now?"

When her lips pulled back, it revealed sharp teeth.

"You can't do anything down there, can you?"

She hissed.

Teetering on the edge of the opening was a lump of reinforced concrete that was almost as big as the girl. Thank god that hadn't fallen in when he was down there, he thought. Sidestepping around the hole, Jake watched the thing and she watched him right back.

"You killed my friend, you little bitch." Tears stood in his eyes when he gave the concrete the gentlest shove and it toppled in.

Flinching at the wet crunch, Jake looked down and saw the girl's limbs protruding from beneath the concrete at unnatural angles. Her porcelain appendages with their black veins lay limp. An ever-increasing dark pool spread outwards.

Watching the thick blood coat her skin, Jake kicked more debris in after her, lifted his scarf, and spat into the hole.

"Horrible little shit." Spinning around, he walked away, tears still in his eyes. Surely that would be the last he saw of her. It had to be.

Hopefully Rixon wasn't on her side.

Chapter Thirty-Six

Jake's body was slowly failing as he walked over the craggy ground beneath the dark grey sky. The black of night had come and gone twice since he'd last stopped. If he rested, he wouldn't get back up again.

Wincing against the splints that shot up his shins, he fought to fill his grit-damaged lungs. Each breath drew less air than the last; his vision swimming as he ploughed on. Holding his chest with his left hand, Jake's heart played its increasingly irregular beat against his palm. The wind battered his exposed face and ears

Every time he looked up, he expected to see the tall frame of his friend. Although they often went hours without talking, just knowing there was someone there prevented Jake from feeling lonely. Looking up at the sky as if Tom were watching down, Jake sighed and returned his attention to the ground, carefully mapping out each step.

One step fell into the next as Jake walked with a zombie gait. The momentum of the stumbling trudge, moments away from falling face-first, pushed him on.

Mistaking a sheet of wood for masonry, he stood on it and it shot from beneath him. Fire exploded in his left buttock when he hit the ground; his back arcing, he thrust his stomach towards the sky. Screaming, he rolled around before falling limp.

Jake lay still, his thigh and lower belly held in a nauseating grip that was radiating outwards. Lying helpless and hopeless like a discarded doll, he cried harder than ever.

Engaged in a losing battle with his pain, Jake finally gave up and rested his tired head against a rock. It was the first time he'd laid down since leaving Tom. Sleep wasn't an option without his friend to watch over him, but his safety didn't matter now. There wouldn't be a morning after this slumber.

When he closed his eyes, he saw an image of Rory lying just out of reach of his dad. Clenching his jaw, Jake fought against the aches and lethargy in his body and stood up.

He couldn't control the outcome of his life, but he could control when he gave up.

When he was fully upright, the force of the wind rocked him. Leaning into it, he fell forwards into his weary gait and moved on again.

###

Hours had passed and Jake barely had the strength left to lift each foot. With leaden legs and a heavy heart, he was virtually at a standstill. Dropping his gaze to the floor, he suddenly saw it.

Nestled in a crack, sheltered on all sides from the wind, was the tiniest splash of pink. Forgetting his aches, Jake fell into a crouch and peered into the tiny crevice. A small flower stared back at him, trembling in the diminished breeze. Its green stalk was barely more than an inch long, and its pink petals stretched out from its yellow centre. It looked like a pink daisy. For something so fragile, it had monumental strength. Having fought its way through tons of rubble, it now stood in open defiance of the corporate giant that owned this world. It reached for the sky in a clear act of beautiful rebellion.

After staring at the only other survivor Jake had seen in days, he lifted his face to the grey clouds and said, "This is it, Tom. This is why I didn't want to play the game. I knew nature would win out. Life's too strong."

Leaning over again, he stroked the delicate petals. With the dust and callouses on his hands, it was impossible to feel the tiny flower, but he saw it move against his touch. That was enough.

When a warmth pressed against the back of his head, he pulled back and looked up again. Deferring to the flower's needs, he moved aside and watched it sparkle in the first beam of sunlight he'd seen in years. Staring at the tiny flower, he smiled...

***

Sitting up straight to keep her tired eyes from closing, she continued watching her monitors. Some showed beaches with tanned and toned men being oiled down by scantily clad women. Some showed sports scenes where winning points were being scored in the most dramatic of fashions. The scenes kept changing, the screens blinking from one shot to the next, all of them showing a reality greater than the user could possibly hope to experience unaided.

All except one.

Having locked the screen hours ago, she continued to stare at Jake lying on the floor of the bus. Her boss had gone to lunch that morning, and she was waiting for him to return.

When she finally felt him walk up behind her, she kept her eyes on the image of the broken man.

"Jake Weston." She said it so quietly it sounded like a low growl. "I've been watching this one for a while. There were things keeping him stuck in his negative projection. His imagined best friend. The city he chose to stay in. Some weird creature things following him. As I watched, those things eventually changed, but he still didn't pull out of it."

Her boss's heavy hand rested on her shoulder. "There's nothing you can do for a negative projection, Marie. There's no one thing dragging them down. You could take away every element of their experience, and they'd simply refill it with another miserable projection. Termination is the only way." Laughing, he squeezed his grip. The cruelty in his tone sent a cold chill running through her. "At least you've popped your cherry. Your first termination is a big deal."

When her boss leaned forward, the smell of his morning coffee and fried food filled her space. As his fat arm stretched over her, she wanted to grab it, but she didn't have the authority to question his decision.

Clasping her hands to stop them from doing anything stupid, she watched her boss double tap the screen and press his thumb against it when he was prompted for his fingerprint.

A panel of buttons filled her monitor. She knew of them only by reputation. There was just one she cared about. It was a big red cross in the centre of the screen.

As if in slow motion, her boss moved towards it, his index finger outstretched.

With her stomach churning and her heart beating in her throat, she watched his pudgy finger. Seconds before he pressed it, she closed her eyes, her entire frame sagging.

I'm sorry, Jake. I'm so sorry.

The flower continued to bask in its spotlight of sun and Jake watched it with a wide grin stretching across his face. Dust clung to his tear-dampened cheeks.

Flinching, Jake shook his head and blinked several times.

Then it came again, like a punch on the nose. The Rixon logo.

Shaking his head, Jake felt dizzy.

It flashed through his vision again. *Rixon.*

Every time the black background and red writing shot into view, it was like being kicked in the face. With every flash he flinched and looked at the Rixon Tower. It changed form, widening and shrinking as if it were being sucked into the ground.

Rixon.

A loud and continuous tone went off in his head. It was deep, shaking his vision as it reverberated through his skull. Everything spun; the outer edges of Jake's world turning the fastest, the horizon now nothing more than a blur. It was like being in the eye of a storm. He looked down at the flower. It was the only thing in the world not spinning. It was resolute and in control. It was at the centre of the chaos. It was the ringmaster, not Jake.

Rixon.

Rixon.

The physics of his world turned on its head and debris and rubbish floated all around him.

Every smell he'd ever experienced hit him in the face and he retched. His nostrils funnelled the sharp rotting tang straight into his body. It felt like being gassed.

Rixon.

Feeling like his stomach had been torn out, Jake stared at his feet.

Rixon.

Rixon.

Rixon.

With wide eyes, he looked out over to where the tower was. All he saw was a grey blur as the horizon whirled faster. The motion made him want to vomit.

Rixon.

Overcome by dizziness and feeling like he'd fall at any second, he shouted, "You fucking arseholes!"

Rixon.

Rixon.

Rixon.

Tom had never existed. Rory had never existed. Thalia had never existed. Nothing was real.

The flashing strobe of the Rixon logo made Jake close his eyes. Unable to stop them, he could at least shut out the desolate world surrounding him.

Then he thought about Tom's theory, which was, in fact, his own. If he experienced it, then it was real. He nodded and raised his voice; his throat wasn't parched anymore.

"Fuck you, Rixon! I've found nature and no matter what you do, you can't take that away from me."

The logo stayed longer every time it appeared and all of the aches and pains in his body had vanished. His hand was no longer bandaged and there was no sign of injury.

Throwing his middle finger up in the direction of the tower, he continued, "I beat your stupid fucking game!" Looking at the sky again, he said, "I've won, Tom. No matter what they do, they can't take this experience away from me. I perceived it, so that's all that matters, right? You existed. You, Rory, and Thalia were real. *I'm* the one who chooses my reality, not them."

His legs then buckled beneath him and he fell to the side as the Rixon logo dominated his vision for about ten seconds. When the world reappeared, his face was just millimetres from the delicate flower. As he stared at it, the edges of his view darkened and closed in.

Soon, all that was left of the flower was a pinprick of pink. A smile sat on his face. The past several years were real because he'd given them permission to be real.

He'd won.

His world went black.

No sight...

No sound...

No smell...

No taste...

No feeling...

...Logged off.

End

The Ending

Dear Reader,

As a writer, I'm aware that the 'and then it was all a dream' ending can be seen as a cop out, which is why I wanted to take the time to write why I made this choice for the end of *New Reality: Truth.*

Truth is the first book in the series of the New Reality books. It's called Truth because it was written to explore the subjective nature of our own personal realities. It's a look at the idea that regardless of the information in front of us, what becomes our truth, or our reality, is what we choose to accept as such. As Friedrich Nietzsche said, "Nothing is true, everything is permitted." Our reality is what we've chosen it to be. Objectivity is an illusion.

Join The Newsletter:

Want to be the first to know about my latest work and other material? Sign up to my newsletter and get exclusive content only available to newsletter fans. Join for these benefits and more:

- Free stories on signup
- Free regular content
- Advance notice of my latest releases
- Notice of discounts and promotions
- The chance to receive free advanced reader copies in exchange for an honest review
- No spam

Join Today!
www.michaelrobertson.co.uk

Reviews

Reviews are valuable to writers to help increase our visibility.
If you have time to leave a review, please do.
It means a great deal to me.
Thank you.

Michael.

About The Author

Michael Robertson has been a writer for many years and has had poetry and short stories published, most notably with HarperCollins. He first discovered his desire to write as a skinny weed-smoking seventeen-year-old badman who thought he could spit bars over drum and bass. Fortunately, that venture never left his best mate's bedroom and only a few people had to endure his musical embarrassment. He hasn't so much as looked at a microphone since. What the experience taught him was that he liked to write. So that's what he did.

After sending poetry to countless publications and receiving MANY rejection letters, he uttered the words, "That's it, I give up." The very next day, his first acceptance letter arrived in the post. He saw it as a sign that he would find his way in the world as a writer.

Over a decade and a half later, he now has a young family to inspire him and has decided to follow his joy with every ounce of his being. With the support of his amazing partner, Amy, he's managed to find the time to take the first step of what promises to be an incredible journey. Love, hope, and the need to eat get him out of bed every morning to spend a precious few hours pursuing his purpose.

If you want to connect with Michael:

Subscribe to my newsletter at:
http://www.michaelrobertson.co.uk

Email me at:
subscribers@michaelrobertson.co.uk

Follow me on Facebook at:
https://www.facebook.com/MichaelRobertsonAuthor

Twitter at:
@MicRobertson

Google Plus at:
https://plus.google.com/u/0/113009673177382863155/posts

Author's Note

The idea for *New Reality* came to me after reading a comic adaptation of *Philip K. Dick's Electric Ant* by David Mack. The story is of an android discovering he isn't a real person. After plenty of 'soul' searching, the android concludes that its ability to process the world like a human being through sensory receptors makes it living. It permits itself to exist.

This got me thinking. If an entertainment system could stimulate all five of our senses, would it be convincing enough for the user to think it was real? Could it be better than reality? What if it responded to desire? Would anyone ever log off?

New Reality is the result of this line of thought.

DEAD ISLAND: Operation Zulu

Ten years after the world was nearly brought to its knees by a zombie Armageddon, there is a race for the antidote! On a remote Caribbean island, surrounded by a horde of hungry living dead, a team of American and Australian commandos must rescue the Antidotes' scientist. Filled with zombies, guns, Russian bad guys, shady government types, serial killers and elevator muzak. Dead Island is an action packed blood soaked horror adventure.

Allen Gamboa

INVASION OF THE DEAD SERIES

On the east coast of Australia, five friends returning from a month-long camping trip slowly discover that a virus has swept through much of the country. What greets them in a gradual revelation is an enemy beyond compare. Armed with dwindling ammunition, the friends must overcome their disagreements, utilize their individual skills, and face unimaginable horrors as they battle to reach their hometown and make sense of life in the new world.

Owen Baillie

SIXTH CYCLE

Nuclear war has destroyed human civilization. Captain Jake Phillips wakes into a dangerous new world, where he finds the remaining fragments of the population living in a series of strongholds, connected across the country. Uneasy alliances have maintained their safety, but things are about to change. -- **Discovery leads to danger.** -- Skye Reed, a tracker from the Omega stronghold, uncovers a threat that could spell the end for their fragile society. With friends and enemies revealing truths about the past, she will need to decide who to trust. -- **Sixth Cycle** is a gritty post-apocalyptic story of survival and adventure.

<u>Darren Wearmouth</u> ~ <u>Carl Sinclair</u>

SPLINTER

For close to a thousand years they waited, waited for the old knowledge to fade away into the mists of myth. They waited for a re-birth of the time of legend for the time when demons ruled and man was the fodder upon which they fed. They waited for the time when the old gods die and something new was anxious to take their place. **A young couple was all that stood between humanity and annihilation.** Ill equipped and shocked by the horrors thrust upon them they would fight in the only way they knew how, tooth and nail. Would they be enough to prevent the creation of the feasting hordes? Were they alone able to stand against evil banished from hell? **Would the horsemen ride when humanity failed?** The earth would rue the day a splinter group set up shop in Cold Spring.

<u>H. J. Harry</u>

WHISKEY TANGO FOXTROT SERIES

The world is at war with the Primal Virus. Military forces across the globe have been recalled to defend the homelands as the virus spreads and decimates populations. Out on patrol and assigned to a remote base in Afghanistan, Staff Sergeant Brad Thompson's unit was abandoned and left behind, alone and without contact. They survived and have built a refuge, but now they are forgotten. **No contact with their families or commands**. Brad makes a tough decision to leave the safety of his compound to try and make contact with the States, desperate to find rescue for his men. **What he finds is worse than he could have ever predicted**.

W. J. Lundy

13971369R00145

Printed in Great Britain
by Amazon.co.uk, Ltd.,
Marston Gate.